kicking& screaming

THE MOVIE NOVEL

UNIVERSAL PICTURES PRESENTS A MOSAIC MEDIA GROUP PRODUCTION A JESSE DYLAN FILM WILL FERRELL ROBERT DUVALL "KICKING & SCREAMING"
KATE WALSH MIKE DITKA MUSIC BY DAVID NEWMAN COSTUME DESIGNER PAMELA WITHERS CHILTON EDITED BY STUART PAPPÉ PETER TESCHNER PRODUCTION DESIGNER CLAYTON R. HARTLEY
DIRECTOR OF PHOTOGRAPHY LLOYD AHERN ASC EXECUTIVE PRODUCERS CHUCK ROVEN JUDD APATOW DANIEL LUPI PRODUCED BY JIMMY MILLER WRITTEN BY STEVE RUDNICK & LEO BENVENUTI
Mosaic MEDIA GROUP | THIS FILM IS NOT YET RATED | DIRECTED BY JESSE DYLAN www.kickingandscreamingmovie.com A UNIVERSAL PICTURE UNIVERSAL
© 2004 UNIVERSAL STUDIOS

kicking & screaming

THE MOVIE NOVEL

By Susan Korman
Based on the Motion Picture Screenplay
Written by Steve Rudnick & Leo Benvenuti

HarperKidsEntertainment
An Imprint of HarperCollinsPublishers

CHAPTER ONE

The trouble between my dad and Grandpa Buck didn't start with me—or my soccer team. Their problems began way before that, when my dad was just a kid.

Grandpa Buck was so crazy about sports, he used to put a baseball in Dad's crib instead of my father's favorite stuffed rabbit. On Halloween, Dad wasn't allowed to wear a ghost or superhero costume. Grandpa Buck made him dress up as George Halas—the founder, owner, and longtime coach of the Chicago Bears football team.

Once when Dad was about to catch a soccer ball kicked into the stands by the great Brazilian player, Pelé, Grandpa

Buck reached over and snatched it right out of Dad's hands.

It was no wonder that the two of them fought all the time. Grandpa Buck had always been tough on my dad, and he always would be.

My name is Sam Weston. I'm ten years old, and last year I played soccer for the Highland Heights Soccer Organization. And that was when the trouble between my dad and Grandpa Buck really started spinning out of control.

At first I was on Grandpa Buck's team, the Gladiators. And just like when Dad was a kid with Grandpa as his coach, I had spent the whole season, so far, on the bench. Today we were playing the Pythons—one of the toughest teams in the league—and guess where I was. . . .

That's right, on the bench.

The game was almost over, and Grandpa Buck was marching up and down the sideline like a madman. "Come on, Gladiators! Make something happen!" he hollered at the kids on the field. "You have to go *to* the ball—not run away from it! You look like a bunch of wimps out there! Come on! Are you going to let this game end in a tie, or what?"

On the field, Bucky, who was Grandpa Buck's son from his second marriage, gritted his teeth. With a burst of speed, he raced toward a Pythons player and stole the ball. Then he maneuvered around another opponent and ran toward the goal.

"Shoot!" Grandpa Buck shouted. "Close the deal, Bucky!"

I watched Bucky dribble closer to the net. Behind him, a Pythons player had almost caught up.

But Bucky knew the opposing player was there. In the nick of time, he turned his body toward the goal and kicked hard.

The soccer ball slammed into the corner of the net.

"Goal!" A cheer rang out along our sideline.

The Gladiators had taken the lead.

"That's my boy! Way to go, Bucky!" Grandpa Buck shouted.

It's a little weird, but Bucky, who is exactly my age, is my uncle. And when he was born, Grandpa Buck's dream of having a great athlete for a son came true. Unlike Dad and me, Bucky is good at every sport he tries.

A few moments later, the ref blew the whistle. To my relief, the game was finally over.

The other Gladiators surrounded Bucky on the field and began the usual "friendly" cheer for the other team. But I stayed right where I was, slumped on the bench.

Mom and Dad walked over to me slowly, bright smiles painted on their faces.

"So how'd it go, big guy?" Dad called cheerfully.

"Great," I muttered as sarcastically as I could. Then I patted the bench next to me. "See? It's nice and warm."

"Oh, yeah?" Dad had arrived late from work, so he didn't know I'd spent the whole game on the bench again. He frowned and glanced over at Grandpa Buck, who was still leading the cheer for the Pythons. "I'll see what I can do about that," he muttered under his breath.

"Can we go now?" I pleaded. "Please?"

"Sure, honey." Mom put an arm around me, and we started toward the car.

Just then Grandpa Buck looked up and saw us leaving.

My father caught his eye. "We'll see you later, Dad," he called slowly.

Uh-oh, I thought, catching a glimpse of my father's face. That night we were going to Grandpa Buck's house for a barbecue. And judging from Dad's expression, more than the grill would be sizzling.

CHAPTER TWO

Grandpa Buck lives in a huge house in the fancy part of town. The entryway alone is about twice the size of our living room and the backyard has a pool. Janice, Grandpa Buck's young wife, greeted us when we arrived.

"Hi, you guys! Buck!" she called. "They're here!"

Grandpa Buck came to the door in the apron he always wore when he was grilling.

"Hey, hey! Look who's here," he said. He gave Mom and me a hug. Then he started right in giving Dad a hard time. "It's two of my favorite people—and Phil!"

Dad was already scowling. "Very funny, Dad. I never get tired of that one."

Inside the house someone was playing the piano—beautiful classical music.

"Wow," Dad murmured, impressed. "You hired a pianist."

"No." Grandpa Buck shook his head. "That's Bucky."

Bucky?

Dad and I exchanged looks. Bucky really was good at everything he did—not just sports.

As Bucky switched to a swinging jazz number, Grandpa Buck turned to Dad. "You quit piano lessons, didn't you, Phil?"

Dad clenched his teeth. "Yes—I—did, Dad."

"Darn shame," said Grandpa Buck.

Luckily, just then Janice took the bowl Mom was carrying, breaking the tension. "What do you have there?" she asked Mom. "Fruit salad?"

Mom nodded. "I found the juiciest strawberries."

They chatted for a few more minutes. Then Grandpa Buck remembered something.

"Come here," he said to Dad and me. "I have something to show you."

He led us into the den and pointed proudly to the big TV, where a commercial was playing. It was for Buck's Sports Town—Grandpa Buck's chain of sporting goods stores.

I smiled as I watched him mouth along with the words from the commercial.

"And to celebrate the opening of my new store in Tinley Grove, all this month you can save big on any kind of balls. I've got basketballs . . ."

Grandpa Buck suddenly turned toward Dad. "I own four stores now, Phil. I'm opening a fifth next month, in your neck of the woods. You sure you don't want a job?"

My dad owned a health food store, where he sold vitamins and other nutritional items. "I have a job, Dad," he told Grandpa Buck wearily.

"Yeah, you have a job," Grandpa Buck said. "But selling vitamins? What kind of job is that? You can buy vitamins at the supermarket."

"I sell vitamins and health food items," Dad corrected him. "They are good for people. You should take more vitamins."

"I take a vitamin every day. It's called a steak. *Shhh!*" Grandpa Buck motioned for Dad to be quiet and turned back to the TV. "Here comes the best part."

"*So for all your sporting goods needs, come on down to Buck's Sports Town. I'm Buck Weston, and . . .*"

Just then a loud noise coming from outside drowned out the voice on TV.

"Oh boy," I said, immediately recognizing the sound.

Dad recognized it, too. "Here we go again," he murmured.

"Son of a gun!" Grandpa Buck growled. As he raced outside, we hurried after him. But we already knew what we'd see.

Sure enough, leaves were whirling chaotically above the fence that separates Grandpa Buck's house from the one next door. The sound from the leaf blower was deafening.

Grandpa Buck ran toward the fence. "Stop!" he screamed, frantically waving his arms. "Turn that thing off!"

A second later, the sound stopped. Then Grandpa Buck's neighbor popped his head over the fence.

It was Mike Ditka, the famous football coach who had led the 1985 Chicago Bears to a Super Bowl victory. Coach Ditka was a hero to most people around Chicago, but my grandfather hated his guts.

"I've got company, Ditka!" Grandpa Buck bellowed at him. "Can't you do that later?"

Coach Ditka smirked. "I don't think so, Weston," he replied. "I've got lawn work to do."

"Come on, Dad . . ." My father tried to intervene. "Don't you guys ever get sick and tired of all this fighting?"

"Stay out of this," Grandpa Buck warned Dad. He whirled back toward the fence. "Look," he told the coach. "We're trying to have a nice family gathering."

"And I'm trying to clean my yard," Coach Ditka replied.

"No, you're not! You're trying to annoy me!" With that, Grandpa Buck bent down and scooped up piles of leaves. Furiously, he began tossing them into Coach Ditka's yard.

"Hey, knock it off, Weston!" Coach Ditka shouted. He threw back the leaves.

I watched in disbelief as the two of them kept tossing the leaves back and forth. If they were kids at my school, they would have gotten a detention or a phone call home to their parents for acting like this.

At last, Janice stuck her head out the door to say dinner was ready. "Buck! Come on, let's eat."

Reluctantly, Grandpa Buck dropped his handful of leaves. "We'll settle this later, Ditka!"

"You know where I live," Coach Ditka shot back.

As Grandpa Buck stormed off, Dad stood at the fence for a minute, staring at the famous NFL coach.

Coach Ditka edged closer. "You got a problem?" he sneered.

"Nope!" Dad said, spinning around.

I hurried inside after him.

Unlike Grandpa Buck, Dad and I knew better than to mess with a former NFL coach like Mike Ditka!

CHAPTER THREE

After dinner Bucky and I wrestled with Grandpa Buck on the lawn. Wrestling was one of Grandpa Buck's favorite bonding activities. He kept urging me to knock him over.

"Come on, Sam. Dig in!" he told me. "Bring me down!"

"I don't want to bring you down, Grandpa." Helplessly, I looked toward where Dad sat watching us. "Dad! Save me!" I yelled.

Grandpa Buck laughed. "Go ahead, bring him on. He's no help, sonny. Call your mom, too. I'll take them all on!"

After a while, Bucky got tired. He pulled himself up from the grass and sat down next to my father.

"I'll tell you," I heard him say. "Dad is one pretty tough dude."

My father glanced back at the lawn, where I was still trying to fend off Grandpa Buck.

"How do you do it, Bucky?" he asked with a sigh.

"Do what?" Bucky wanted to know.

"Put up with my dad. He drives me crazy."

Bucky scoffed. "He just likes to push your buttons, Phil."

"He just doesn't seem to bother you the way he bothers me," Dad went on.

Bucky shrugged. "Why would he bother me? He's an incredible man. He inspires me."

"But he never lets up. Nothing is ever good enough," Dad went on. "It's all his way or the highway. Doesn't the pressure ever get to you?"

"Nope." Bucky shook his head. "He taught me how to handle the pressure.

"You're a good man, Phil," Bucky added a second

later, "and a good brother. But I wish you wouldn't take everything so seriously."

Dad knew Bucky was right—most of the time he did take Grandpa Buck too seriously. But tonight he couldn't stop himself, especially since I was involved.

He waited until dessert time. Then he took his cake to the trophy room, where Grandpa Buck sat at his desk.

"Hey, Dad. Can I come in? I want to talk to you about something."

Grandpa Buck nodded. "Sure."

"It's about Sam," Dad began cautiously, "and the soccer team. They look really good this year."

"We're two and oh," Grandpa Buck said proudly. "Can't do much better than first place."

"Sam's really enjoying being on a winning team," Dad said. "But . . ."

"Sammy's a good boy," Grandpa Buck put in.

"Yeah." Dad tried again. "Look, Dad, Sam would never say anything . . . and I'd never tell you how to coach . . . but he really wishes he could have a little more playing time."

Grandpa Buck put down his plate. "Close the door."

Dad did what he asked. "What's up?"

"I'm glad to hear Sam wants more playing time," Grandpa Buck said. "I've already taken care of it."

Dad was confused. "What do you mean?"

"I traded him to the Tigers. He'll get a lot more playing time on that team."

My father's jaw dropped. "You traded him? You traded your own grandson to another team?"

"I didn't really trade him," Grandpa Buck explained quickly. "I mean, I didn't get anything for him. The Tigers lost a kid. So they need another player."

Dad stared at him in disbelief. "That still doesn't tell me why."

"It's because I love him, son. Sam's in over his head on the Gladiators, and it's breaking my heart. At best, he's a benchwarmer on my team."

"A benchwarmer on your team?" Dad echoed.

"That's right." Grandpa Buck nodded. "And you remember how painful that was for you?"

"Yes, I do," Dad managed to reply.

"Is that what you want for your son, Phil?"

At that, Dad whirled around furiously.

Suddenly I heard him bellowing through the house. "Barbara! Sam! Come on. We're going home!"

CHAPTER FOUR

On the car ride home Dad was still steaming. But I didn't know yet what he was so mad about. Besides, he was always furious after spending time with Grandpa Buck.

He turned the car into our driveway.

"Hey, buddy, we'll be right in," he said to me. "Mommy and I would like a little adult time. You know, boring talk."

As soon as I was out of earshot, Dad turned to Mom—and exploded.

"*Benchwarmer?!* Sam's only going to be a benchwarmer on his team? Of all the crazy things my father has ever done, this is the craziest. I mean . . . I know he's the most competitive human being in the world, but this . . . this beats them all!

"I am angry! Spitting angry!" he railed on. "I am a *tornado* of anger!"

Mom, meanwhile, stayed very calm. "I'm glad this happened," she said as soon as Dad let her get in a word.

"You're glad?" He blinked in surprise. "Who are you again?"

"I'm glad it happened," she repeated. "I was always against Sam's playing on your father's team. At least now he's out from under Buck's tyranny."

"What?" Dad stared at her. "Where is my wife?"

"Phil, I'm upset, too," she explained. "But we have to find the positive in this situation. Playing for your dad was unhealthy for Sam. He'll play for another team and finally have some fun.

"You're too upset," she went on. "I'll tell Sam about the new team."

"No." Dad shook his head. "I'll tell him. I know what I'm doing."

Mom looked at him, still uncertain.

"Honesty is always the best policy," Dad said firmly. "He's a tough kid. He can handle it."

I was in my room playing a computer game when Dad came in. I could tell right away that something was up.

"Hey, buddy." He picked up a soccer ball and nervously began bouncing it off his knee. "What are you up to? Creating computer viruses? Hacking into the U.S. Defense Department?" he joked.

I stared at him and waited.

"What is it, Dad?"

"I've got great news!" he said in his phony cheerful voice. "I got you moved to a different soccer team!"

"What?" I didn't know what he was talking about. "I'm not on the Gladiators anymore?"

"No. Guess what? I got you switched to the Tigers!" He made a dumb growling sound, like a tiger.

"The Tigers?" I moaned. "They're awful, Dad! They're in last place."

"Yeah, *now* they're in last place." He tried to be positive. "That's because they didn't have you. It's going to be so much better," he went on. "You'll get way more playing time on this team."

I folded my arms and glared at him. "Grandpa traded me, didn't he?"

"No!" Dad quickly denied it. "No! *Nooooo!*"

Dad was so adamant, I knew I'd guessed right.

I hung my head. "I disappointed Grandpa Buck, didn't I?"

He tried a different tactic. "Hey, soccer is not about pleasing your grandfather. It's about having fun, hanging out with friends, getting some fresh air, and learning about teamwork."

"Grandpa said winning is not the most important thing; it's the *only* thing," I murmured.

"Oh yeah?" Dad shot back. "Well, let me tell you a little secret about your grandfather. A little secret that parents never tell children because if they knew it, it would disrupt our entire civilization!"

That perked up my interest. "Okay. Tell me."

"Sometimes parents are wrong. Sometimes . . . they don't know what they are talking about. Sometimes . . . ," by now Dad was whispering like a crazy person, "parents are just making up real answers because they don't know the answers but they don't want you to think they don't know the answers.

Or sometimes, as in your grandpa's case, they are so sure they have the right answer, they can't see the truth that is right in front of their stupid, shiny bald—"

"So does this mean I don't have to listen to you anymore?" I cut in, trying to stop the tirade.

Dad snapped back to reality. "Of course you have to listen to me, Sam. I'm your father." Then he put an arm around me. "This is going to be great, son. I promise." He did that stupid growl again. "Go . . . Tigers!"

CHAPTER FIVE

"Coach Benson really knows his stuff," Dad said a few days later as the two of us headed toward the soccer fields. It was the first time I'd be playing with my new team.

"This whole thing with Grandpa's trading you to the Tigers will probably end up being a blessing in disguise," he went on.

"I'm not so sure about that," I muttered.

Dad stopped to watch a bunch of kids in green soccer uniforms expertly passing the ball back and forth.

"Hey, look at that, Sam!" Dad exclaimed. "I know the Tigers are in last place, but they look pretty good to me!"

I rolled my eyes at him. "Those are the Pythons, Dad. The Tigers are over there." I pointed to the kids in the orange uniforms hanging out by the field house.

One kid was digging in the dirt with a stick. Another boy had stuffed a soccer ball inside his shirt and was strutting around as if he were pregnant. Most of the other kids were pretending to have sword fights with sticks.

"Oh." Dad didn't know what to say as he took in the scene. "Well, it certainly looks like a nice group of boys."

When we drew closer to the Tigers players, I realized that some of the parents were clustered together, talking in hushed tones.

"Excuse me," Dad called out. "Does anyone know where we can find Coach Benson?"

A few parents looked embarrassed as they shook their heads.

One of the dads waved to me. "Hey, Sam, welcome to the team."

"We haven't seen Coach Benson," one of the moms told Dad, "but . . ." She lowered her voice. "There are lots of rumors going around about him."

"There's a moving van in front of his house," someone else

said. "I think his wife kicked him out."

"I heard he won the lottery," another parent noted.

The parents were still gossiping about Coach Benson when the referee walked over.

"All right, Tigers," he called. "It's game time."

"But our coach isn't here yet," Dad protested.

The ref scowled. "Well, then one of you will have to coach. No coach, no game. That's rule forty-seven, paragraph three: 'All teams must be represented by a bona fide adult coach prior to and during all games,'" he recited.

"Yes, but Coach Benson isn't—" Dad tried again.

"Hey, I don't make up the rules. I just enforce them," the ref interrupted. "You got a problem, take it up with the soccer board. Now get a coach or the Tigers will have to forfeit."

The parents all looked at one another.

"No can do," said Jim, the man in the captain's hat. "I'm putting in fourteen-hour days. I'm Captain Jim, the captain of Captain's Car and Home Audio."

"I just got laid off," another dad murmured.

"I'm a big fan of the game, but I know nothing about it," another parent said.

"I just don't want to coach," admitted somebody else.

"Okay, let's forfeit," said a dad named Forest. "Same time next week, everybody?"

The parents started to scatter.

I was furious. "Great team, Dad," I said sarcastically. "I'm so glad I got traded. Let's go," I added, turning around and starting toward the car.

"Wait!" he blurted out. "I'll coach."

I stopped and looked at him. "You will?"

"Wow, that's great!" several parents said at once. "Thanks. We really appreciate it!"

"It's just one game." Dad went on. "No big deal."

I was thrilled. At least I would get to play soccer today.

A mom handed Dad a thick stack of papers. "Here's Hunter's medical information," she said before running off to join the other parents in the stands.

Dad stared down at the paperwork in his hands. "What is all this stuff?" he asked, looking a little panicked. "What am I supposed to do?"

The other kids and I just stood there, staring at him expectantly.

"Uh . . . well . . ." Dad fumbled. "Let's introduce ourselves and then—"

"Game time!" the ref called out loudly.

"Who are we playing?" Dad asked. But before the ref answered, Dad glanced across the field. "Oh, great," he muttered.

My heart sunk. Standing at midfield, looking ready for another victory, were Grandpa Buck and the Gladiators.

CHAPTER SIX

Grandpa Buck squinted at Dad from the center of the field. "What are you doing here, Phil?" he called. "Where's Benson?"

"Benson's a no-show," I heard Dad explain. He ran over to join Grandpa on the field. "I'm coaching the Tigers today."

"Really?" Grandpa Buck frowned. "You sure you want to do this, Phil?"

Before Dad could answer, the ref started laying out the rules.

"Okay, men. I run a clean game. No arguing, no fighting,

no cursing at the other team. When I make a call, it's official. Have your players take the field."

I saw Dad swallow hard. "Okay." Then he looked at Grandpa Buck. "Good luck, Dad. May the best man win."

"Oh, he will," Grandpa Buck retorted confidently.

Dad jogged back to our sideline. "I want my starters on the field."

"We don't have starters," said a kid named Conner. "We never got that far with Coach Benson. But I usually play goalie."

"Well, then." Dad began pointing out players. "You, you, you, you."

"Me?" Mark, the boy who'd stuffed the ball up his shirt earlier, looked surprised.

"No!" said Dad emphatically. "Not you." He pointed to a few more kids, including me. "You guys. Take the field."

Mark took his spot on the bench behind Dad.

"This will be good," Dad called over his shoulder.

"They're going to kill us, you know," Mark replied.

"Excuse me?" said Dad.

"We're going to get killed," Mark clarified.

Dad nodded. He knew it, too.

The ref blew the whistle to start the game. Within minutes a Gladiator had the ball. He zipped up the field past two of our players, Ambrose and Byong Sun, who stood there watching him race by.

"Don't just stand there, boys! Play!" yelled Dad.

One Tiger started after the ball—and tripped. Another kid wasn't even looking at the ball; he was too busy chasing a butterfly.

The Gladiators player easily made it up the field with the ball. Then he kicked it hard at the net.

Our goalie, Conner, tried hard to make the save. But instead of diving at the ball, he lunged in the opposite direction. I groaned as the ball sailed into the net behind him.

"Goal!" Grandpa Buck yelled triumphantly.

Gladiators, 1; Tigers, 0.

After the goal, I kicked off. This time our team had possession of the ball for a full minute before a Gladiators player stole it away. And then it was Bucky's turn to shoot and score.

The Gladiators' fans went crazy on the sidelines, celebrating.

Bucky ran up to me. "Don't feel bad that we're winning, Sam," he teased. "Maybe it's just that I have a better coach!"

I didn't know what to say to that.

On our sideline, Dad was already hanging his head, while across the field Grandpa Buck was confidently calling out commands to his squad.

"Midfielders, hold it there! Defense! Don't let them out. Slip it easy. Keep it on the ground."

Things quickly went from bad to worse. Ambrose got the ball and kicked it way out-of-bounds. Then he and a kid named Jack collided and fell to the ground, where Hunter then tripped over both of them.

Dad was watching all this, shaking his head, when Mom hurried up to him.

"So it's true?" she said, grinning. "You're the new Tigers coach?"

"It's just for one game, Barbara," he murmured.

"You look good." She gave him a kiss on his cheek. "But shouldn't you be hollering stuff like your dad is doing?"

He nodded. "Okay, midfielders, hold it there!" he yelled, echoing Grandpa Buck. "Slip it easy! Keep it on the ground!"

Mom laughed. "Do you even know what any of that means?"

"I know what 'keep it on the ground' means," Dad told her defensively.

"Well, good luck, honey," Mom said. "Show them what you're made of!"

On the field a kid was running at top speed—away from the ball.

"Where are you going?" Dad shouted at him. "The ball is in play at the other end!"

"That's Hunter," Mark said from the bench. "He's sort of in his own world."

"Oh." Dad turned to look at Mark. "Do you want to go in?"

Mark shook his head. "No. I'm fine here."

Finally, the ref blew the whistle to end the first half.

I grabbed my water bottle, and then collapsed onto the grass around Dad with the rest of the team.

No wonder the Tigers are in last place, I thought glumly. *Everybody on this team stinks!*

Meanwhile, Dad tried to give us a pep talk.

"Now I saw some great playing out there. Lots of good effort. Powerful kicking, Ambrose. And you, Hunter, my friend, you have got some real speed. All in all, a great job out there."

My jaw dropped. Everyone else stared at him in disbelief.

"Hey, coach." Ambrose spoke up, asking the question on everybody's mind. "Are you sure you were watching the same game?"

When the match against the Gladiators finally ended, I had no idea what the final score was. I didn't want to know.

But I did know that our team hadn't scored a single goal.

The Gladiators stood on the field giving us the "friendly" cheer.

"Two, four, six, eight.
Who do we appreciate?
Tigers! Tigers!
Yay, Tigers!"

When Dad returned the equipment to the field house, the woman who worked there shook her head at him.

"I've been here twelve years," she said. "That was one of the worst games I've ever seen."

"Thank you, Patty," muttered Dad. "Thank you very much."

Just then Grandpa Buck approached, carrying his equipment.

"Hey, Buck," Patty called. "Looking good out there."

"You said it!" Grandpa Buck replied. Then he looked at Dad. "Tough game today, huh?"

"We did okay."

Grandpa Buck shrugged. "I told my boys to go easy, but when they see an empty net, they're like animals."

"All right, Dad," my father snapped. "That's enough, okay?"

I followed them as they walked toward the parking lot.

"I heard Coach Benson is gone," Grandpa Buck said. He glanced quickly at Dad. "What do you say I take Sam back? He'll be on a winning team. He'll get a trophy. So what if he's a benchwarmer?"

"No." Dad stopped and took a deep breath. "No. He won't be a benchwarmer. Not my son. Not on your team. I'm going to coach the Tigers. Sam's going to play, and I'm going to coach him."

"Ouch." Grandpa Buck grimaced as if he were in pain.

"Ouch? Why ouch?" Dad demanded.

"Nothing," Grandpa Buck said.

"You get pleasure out of seeing me fail, don't you, Dad?"

"Hey, succeed at something and give me an option," Grandpa Buck replied.

"I am succeeding at selling vitamins," Dad shot back. "And I will succeed at coaching, too!"

"You always think you know better than your old man, huh, Philly boy? I guess you just want to raise yourself."

"I'm thirty-six years old," Dad reminded him. "I already raised myself, and I did a good job!"

Grandpa Buck shook his head. "You're talking half-cocked . . ."

I stood there while the two of them argued back and forth for a few more minutes.

"You really think you can coach in my league?" Grandpa Buck finally demanded.

Dad nodded. "I certainly do—and I'll see you on the field!" With that, he stalked off toward our car.

"Be forewarned, muchacho!" Grandpa Buck yelled after him. "This is the Highland Heights Soccer Organization. You're in the big show now!"

CHAPTER SEVEN

D ad spent the next few days holed up inside his bedroom. He was studying soccer books and watching a soccer training video called *Kickin' It*, hosted by some guy named Soccer Dan.

Whenever Mom or I tried to talk to Dad, he waved us away. All he could think about was proving to Grandpa Buck that he could coach my soccer team.

As soon as Dad and I arrived at the park for soccer practice a few days later, Byong Sun's mother, Ann, hurried over. She handed Dad a book titled *My Child Is Shy*.

"Byong Sun is very quiet," she said nervously. "This book

really helped us deal with it. You should probably give it a once-over."

"I absolutely will," Dad said.

She handed another book to him. This one was called *My Child Is Adopted.*

"I'll read this one, too," he promised.

When all the players were there, Dad gathered us together on the bleachers. "Okay, Tigers. I have some very exciting news." Dad proudly puffed up his chest. "Guess what. You are looking at your new full-time soccer coach."

I don't know what he was expecting, but no one said a word. Maybe they were all as nervous as I was about this news.

"You may be interested to know that I played in this same league as a child," he went on brightly. "And although I haven't played soccer in some twenty-five years, I think you'll find that I still know my way around the old . . . er . . ."—he fumbled for the word—"goalposts. And now . . ." He moved to one side to reveal something behind him. "I have a surprise for you."

It was a table crowded with vitamins and protein shakes.

Now I was really embarrassed. "Dad," I warned him in a low voice. "Don't push the vitamins."

"I don't have to push the vitamins, Sam," he said proudly. "The vitamins push themselves."

"I'm begging you," I pleaded. "Please put them away."

But Dad wasn't listening.

"You're all going to love this. Everyone on this team will get a free month of supplements. And I'd like to start each practice with these protein shakes. Everyone, come get one."

Reluctantly we stood, and Dad started handing out bottles of the disgusting-looking drink.

"Yuck!" Ambrose peered into his bottle. "Mine has chunks in it."

"It looks like puke!" Conner said.

"It's not puke, Conner," Dad said patiently. "It's protein. And when you run out, stop by my store and I'll replenish your supply."

"Hey!" Something suddenly occurred to Conner. "Can we get free stuff from your dad's store, too?"

Dad frowned. "I don't think so." He changed the subject. "Now my philosophy on coaching is—"

"Can you at least get us a discount at Buck's Sports Town?" Conner persisted.

Dad sighed. "I'll see what I can do."

"How much of a discount do you think?" Conner wanted to know.

"I can't get anyone a discount!" Dad finally snapped. "What I'd really like to do is talk about my philosophy on coaching. Now I believe that a coach's responsibility—"

Mark raised his hand. "Hey, coach. Remember when Conner asked you for a discount at your dad's awesome store?"

"Yes." Dad squinted at him. "That just happened."

"Yeah," Mark went on. "Remember?"

Dad was getting impatient. "I remember," he said. "Now . . ."

"Ha!" Mark started laughing. "Got you good! Call the burn unit!"

Dad just stared at him. "That wasn't funny—or clever."

"It was to me!" Mark said.

This time everyone laughed.

"All right. That's enough," Dad said sharply. "I would really like to talk about my philosophy about winning and losing. I believe that the most important thing is playing the game and having fun."

"Losing is not fun," the shy boy, Byong Sun, pointed out.

"That's true," Dad replied. "But—"

Just then Hunter stepped up and gave Dad a note. "It's from my mom," he explained.

Dad opened it and read: *Please don't let Hunter anywhere near anything containing sugar.*

"Hunter," Dad said, noticing big brown splotches on the note. "There's chocolate all over this thing."

"I know." Hunter looked sheepish. "I have a problem, coach. I'm not denying it. It's a real problem, and I'm owning that."

"Okay, calm down," Dad told him. "From here on in, just lay off the sweets."

Hunter hesitated. "I'll try," he said finally. "But there are no guarantees in life. All I can do is try."

"Okay then, Tigers," Dad went on, "it's time to stop talking and start playing. You have yet to win a game this season, which is fine, but we have some work to do. Here's how we'll do it. . . .

"When I blow the whistle once, it means come off the field. When I blow the whistle twice, it means come on it. And three blasts on the whistle—"

I couldn't take it anymore. "Dad!"

"Okay." To my relief, Dad dropped the whole whistle thing. "I think this talk went really well," he said, beaming at us. "Take the field, everybody, and let's play!"

After that, things went downhill pretty fast. Dad spent the next hour shouting instructions at us—everything he'd learned from watching Soccer Dan and reading the stack of soccer books.

"Move the ball down the field!"

"Use the inside of your foot!"

"Kick it hard!"

"Make contact in the upper quadrant of the ball!"

"Don't use your hands!"

Unfortunately, the Tigers had a very different approach to playing soccer.

While Dad tried to "train" us, Ambrose lay on the field watching the clouds. Byong Sun played with sticks. Jack tried to eat a grasshopper, and when Hunter wasn't stuffing the ball up under his shirt, he was busy climbing trees. Worst of all, our goalie, Conner, couldn't seem to even get close to the ball when he was trying to make a save.

Finally, after Byong Sun nearly poked out Mark's eye with a stick, I saw my father sag in defeat.

I walked over to him.

"I think I need help, Sam," he murmured.

I nodded my agreement.

The truth was pretty clear. Even with expert tips from Soccer Dan, Dad was in way over his head.

CHAPTER EIGHT

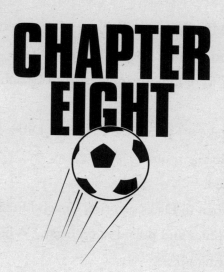

I have to say, my father's next move was brilliant. As soon as Dad realized he needed help, he drove over to Grandpa Buck's neighborhood. But he wasn't there to visit my grandfather.

Instead he pulled up at the house next door—Coach Ditka's house.

Mrs. Ditka led him into the den. It was a large room decorated with frilly drapes, doilies on the furniture, dozens of Beanie Babies, and fancy throw pillows.

"Be a honey and take off your shoes," Mrs. Ditka told him. "I'll go get Mike."

"Thanks, Mrs. Ditka."

Dad looked around. Behind Mrs. Ditka's collection of Beanie Babies were lots of trophies from Coach Ditka's days in the NFL.

"Did you take off your shoes?" Coach Ditka asked as soon as he came into the room.

Dad nodded.

"Good." Then to Dad's surprise, Coach Ditka reached into one of the trophies and pulled out a cigar. "What's up, Paul?" he asked, lighting up.

"My name is Phil, not Paul," Dad corrected him.

"It's not Paul?"

"No, it's Phil."

Coach Ditka shrugged. "What's the difference? What do you want, anyway? Come on. Spit it out."

"Okay," Dad started. "Here it is."

"Mike!" Mrs. Ditka suddenly yelled from another room. "Are you smoking in there?"

"Hold this!" Coach Ditka shoved the cigar at Dad as his wife hurried into the room.

She frowned at Dad. "We don't allow smoking in this house," she said sternly.

He flushed. "Oh, sorry, Mrs. Ditka."

Coach Ditka took the cigar from him. "I'll get rid of it," he promised his wife.

As soon as Mrs. Ditka was gone, the coach started smoking again.

Dad went back to trying to explain the Tigers' situation. "So I'm coaching my son's soccer team, and I was wondering if you'd like to help me."

"Soccer?" Coach Ditka made a face.

"Yes. It's a good group of boys. Ten- to twelve-year-olds."

"You want me to coach a bunch of ten- to twelve-year-old soccer players?" Coach Ditka said. He went over to the window to blow out the smoke.

"Actually . . . I want you to be my *assistant* coach," Dad clarified.

"Assistant coach?" Coach Ditka spun toward him. "Do you have any idea who I am?" he boomed.

Dad backed right down. "It was a silly idea," he said nervously. "It's just . . . I need help. I know that you're a great coach, Mike, and . . . well, my dad's going to ride me pretty hard during the season. I—"

"Wait a minute." Coach Ditka blinked as Dad's words sunk

in. "Did I hear you right? I'd be coaching against your dad?"

Dad nodded. "Well, yes."

Coach Ditka grinned in delight. "Why didn't you say so in the first place?"

"Mike!" Mrs. Ditka suddenly yelled from another room. "I smell smoke!"

"Nobody's smoking!" Coach Ditka yelled back. Then he clapped Dad on the back. "So it's you and me against your dad, huh?"

"Well, there are some other teams, too," Dad explained hastily. "But . . ."

His words trailed off as Mrs. Ditka stepped into the room and glared at her husband. "Mike . . ."

"I know," he mumbled. "No smoking means no smoking." With that, he tossed the cigar out the window.

Then he looked back at Dad. "I'm in," he said, grinning broadly again. "Let's bring him down!"

When Dad and I arrived at the soccer field with Coach Ditka for the Tigers' next game, the parents and kids were waiting on the sideline. Dad couldn't wait to tell everybody the big news.

"Okay, Tigers!" he called eagerly. "Look who's here with me!"

The kids just stared blankly. But some of the parents recognized Coach Ditka right away.

"Conner." His father nudged him. "You know who that is?"

"No." Conner shook his head. He didn't have a clue.

Mark's father stepped up close to the famous NFL coach and started videotaping him.

Coach Ditka was annoyed. He pushed the camera back at Mark's dad. "You want to get that out of my face?"

"No problem, sir!" he apologized.

"Come on, Tigers." Dad prodded them again. "I'll give you a hint about this man. Think Hall of Fame. Chicago Bears."

Mark raised his hand. "Is he Sammy Sosa?"

Dad shook his head. "Wrong sport. Think football. He led the 1986 Bears—"

"Eighty-*five*," Coach Ditka corrected him.

"He led the eighty-five Bears to a Super Bowl victory," Dad went on.

The kids were still staring blankly.

Wisely, Dad gave up. "Okay. I'll tell you. This man is . . . Mike Ditka!"

Knowing his name didn't help. None of the kids reacted.

Finally, Mark raised his hand. "Do you at least know Sammy Sosa?" he asked the football coach.

"Mike Ditka is a great coach," Dad broke in. "And guess what? He's going to be my assistant!"

Mark raised his hand again. "If he's so great," he said suspiciously, "then why isn't he the *head* coach?"

"Hey, kid, can it!" Coach Ditka snarled. "I'm a coach who doesn't give up! From now on, your entire lives are going to be about winning. You're going to eat, breathe, and sleep winning!"

Mark suddenly looked nervous.

"I am going to push you like no man has ever pushed you before. You'll curse the day I was born!" Coach Ditka boomed. He went on and on.

"At times you'll wish I was dead. So if you're not up to the challenge, I recommend you get off this field right now, because I eat quitters for breakfast and spit out their bones. I am the law. This is going to be the hardest, most painful thing you'll attempt in your entire lives, but when it is done, you'll be champions. For the love of Pete, you'll be champions!"

I was impressed—and suddenly feeling a little more

optimistic about my new team.

"He's good," I whispered to Dad.

He nodded back at me.

"Hands in, Tigers!" Coach Ditka shouted. "Now let's get out there and kick some butt!"

We gathered around Dad and Coach Ditka and put our hands in the middle of the circle.

"Okay, Tigers," Dad said. "On three, shout, 'Let's have fun.' One . . . two . . . three!"

"Let's have fun!" we all yelled obediently.

But as soon as the starters ran onto the field, I saw Coach Ditka shoot Dad a look.

"'Let's have fun?'" he echoed, shaking his head. "Come on, Weston. What kind of message is that?"

CHAPTER NINE

Today we were playing the Tarantulas.

It took only a few minutes for Jack to lose the ball, and then only a few more minutes for the Tarantulas to score an easy goal.

Coach Ditka started pacing along the sideline.

"They're just warming up," Dad said quickly. "Getting into the flow."

Right after the kickoff, we lost possession again. A Tarantulas player dribbled the ball up the field toward Ambrose, who stood alone in the center of the field.

"Let me see some hustle, Ambrose!" Coach Ditka yelled.

But Ambrose barely moved. Instead he just sauntered toward the ball.

"You're moving like a bear, Ambrose!" his father screamed. "Pick up the pace!"

Coach Ditka popped gum into his mouth and spun toward Dad. "Why aren't they staying with the ball?"

"Well . . ." Dad couldn't exactly explain it. "We did work on . . ."

Just then the Tarantulas scored again.

"Come on, Conner!" Now the goalie's father was mad. "You dove in the wrong direction! You've got to keep your eyes on the ball!"

Coach Ditka snapped his gum furiously and spun toward my father. "These kids are terrible, Phil!" he declared. "You didn't tell me they were this bad. You should have told me."

"Mike," Dad said nervously. "They're kids. You really should calm down."

"Can't anybody here play this game?" hollered Coach Ditka, throwing his clipboard onto the ground.

Meanwhile, Ambrose had managed to stop the ball in front

of the Tarantulas' net. He made a soft kick toward the goal.

The Tarantulas' goalie scooped it up.

Ambrose turned toward the sideline and shrugged. "I gave it my best shot," he said to no one in particular.

The goalie tossed the ball back into play. It smacked Ambrose on the back of the head and ricocheted off to the side.

Just then Hunter bent down to pick up a piece of candy he'd spotted on the field.

Smack!

The ball hit Hunter in the backside and then, to everyone's amazement, bounced right into the net.

"Goal!" I screamed, jumping up and down in excitement. "We scored a goal!"

While all the Tigers on the field whooped and celebrated, the Tarantulas stood and watched.

"What are they celebrating for?" I heard one kid ask.

"It's their first goal of the season," another player replied.

"Whoop-de-doo," the other replied, unimpressed.

But Dad was pretty excited, too. "Hey!" he called to Coach Ditka. "We scored a goal!"

"That wasn't a goal," Coach Ditka fired back. "That was a train wreck!"

After completely annihilating our team, the Tarantulas gathered to give us the "friendly" cheer.

"Two, four, six, eight.

Who do we appreciate?

Tigers! Tigers!

Yay, Tigers!"

Coach Ditka was furious. "What the heck are those kids cheering about?" he demanded. "We ought to go over there and bust some heads!"

"It's a kids' league, Mike," Dad had to explain. "They're just showing their appreciation for our hard effort. Maybe we should give them a cheer back."

"You cheer, Phil!" Coach Ditka snapped. "The rest of us have work to do!"

CHAPTER TEN

Coach Ditka ran the next few practices. We all found out pretty quickly why he had earned a reputation for being a tough coach.

I had never been so exhausted. Coach Ditka made us do push-ups, sprints, and drills using a blocking sled—special equipment used by football players. Whenever we made a mistake or complained about how hard he was working us, he got in our faces and screamed. He didn't care that we were kids; he just kept shouting insults at us at the top of his lungs.

Meanwhile, Dad kept trying to encourage everyone. One day he went into a toy shop to look for gifts for us.

"Excuse me," he said to a clerk, "do you have any of those blank award certificates?"

"They're in the back, by the birds."

Dad was searching the aisle when something caught his eye—a little bird toy that chirped when it was wound up.

That, unfortunately, gave him an idea.

At the next practice he stood in front of us. "I have something for each of you to thank you for all your hard work."

I stared in disbelief as he showed us what he'd bought: a bird for each us—a real finch—inside a small birdcage.

Ambrose did a double take. "You bought us birds?"

Dad nodded proudly.

"I don't get it. Why is that fun?" Ambrose asked.

"Do we have to keep them?" Conner wanted to know.

"You *get* to keep them," Dad said, still oblivious to everyone's lack of enthusiasm. "This is my way of saying thanks. Great job, boys."

Byong Sun leaned down and slowly opened his birdcage. Immediately the finch flew away.

"I got extras!" Dad reassured him.

Coach Ditka was watching Dad and shaking his head.

"You're a master motivator, Phil," he said sarcastically. "From now on, let me show you how it's done in the big leagues."

"Focus, Mark!" his father yelled in frustration as he watched us play the Lightning Bolts. "Stop fooling around!"

"Move, Ambrose!" His father was yelling, too. "Good, now pick up the pace!"

The Lightning Bolts scored several more times.

"Good job, Conner!" his dad called. "You got a *little* closer to the ball that time."

Coach Ditka stalked up and down the sideline like a lion, with Dad shadowing him constantly.

At halftime Coach Ditka drew up a complicated plan on a dry-erase board and showed it to us.

I nodded along with everyone else as he barked complicated directions at us. But none of us had a clue what he was talking about. When we ran back onto the field to execute the play, we all ran in different directions. Then we shot aggressively, just like Coach Ditka had said to do, only we scored in the other team's goal.

I ran up the field to challenge the Lightning Bolts player who had the ball. He faked me out, and I fell to the ground.

A second later, he scored.

"Sam! Get back in the play!" Mom screamed at me from the stands. "Stay with the ball. Phil, tell him!"

Suddenly, Jack had the ball. Quickly, he moved it down the field. When he reached the goal, he looked around nervously and then kicked hard. To everyone's shock, it soared past the goalie and slammed into the net.

We all began celebrating.

"Now that was a goal!" Coach Ditka yelled. "That was a real goal!"

On the sidelines the parents were jumping up and down, hugging one another.

"Did that just happen?" one of the moms shouted. "Was that really a goal?"

"Two, four, six, eight.
Who do we appreciate?
Tigers! Tigers!
Yay, Tigers!"
The Tigers had lost again.

Coach Ditka slammed his clipboard onto the ground. "That's enough!" he shouted at the Lightning Bolts players.

"Easy, Mike." Dad tried to calm him.

"I don't want their appreciation!" he screamed. "I want to win! Shut your mouths!" he yelled to the chanting kids.

Instantly, they stopped, terrified.

As Coach Ditka stomped off toward his car, I watched him go. Then I noticed Grandpa Buck and the Gladiators players, who were waiting to take the field for their game.

Grandpa Buck had spotted Dad and was giving him a big wave.

But my father turned around and didn't wave back.

CHAPTER ELEVEN

That night, the parents and coaches went to the annual Highland Heights Soccer Organization dinner, which was held at a popular steak house in town.

Mom and Dad told me that Grandpa Buck ran the show. No surprise there.

"Evening, folks," Grandpa Buck said into the microphone. "I want to welcome you to tonight's dinner. This event is sponsored by Buck's Sports Town, and you know me, I'm . . ."

My parents rolled their eyes as Grandpa Buck went on talking about himself and his successful chain of stores.

At last he changed the subject.

"Every year we like to take a little time for the coaches to come up here and tell us a little about their teams. Hey, I'll go first," he added with a grin. "My Gladiators are in first place, and we're going to stay there!"

Parents of the Gladiators clapped loudly while some others booed playfully.

"All right, settle down," Grandpa Buck said, still grinning. "You're all just jealous. Now I'm going to bring up someone who's new to coaching in this league but close to me. I love him like a son. My oldest boy, Phil. Come on up, Phil."

Dad groaned. Reluctantly, he climbed to his feet and made his way to the stage area up front.

At the microphone, he wasn't sure what to say.

"Uh . . . well . . . I'm Phil Weston . . . and I'm coaching the Tigers. And we're a team with . . . uh, a lot of potential. In fact, we scored a goal today—a real goal. So the Tigers are a team on the way up. And . . . well, I wasn't expecting to speak tonight. I was . . . er . . . hoping that my assistant coach would be here to . . ."

Just then the door opened, and a huge figure stepped into the back of the room.

"Ah! He just arrived!" Dad exclaimed happily. "Ladies and

gentlemen, it gives me great pleasure to introduce my assistant coach, Hall of Fame player and coach—Mike Ditka!"

"Mike Ditka?" Grandpa Buck echoed. "But . . . but . . ." He was seething.

The crowd burst into applause. Then everyone, except Grandpa Buck, stood to get a better look at the famous NFL coach.

Coach Ditka made his way to the front of the room and joined Dad.

"Thanks, everyone," he said into the microphone. "I'm happy to be here."

Grandpa Buck sneered. "You live long enough, you see everything. 'Iron' Mike and 'Aluminum' Phil coaching the Tigers!"

"What was that, Weston?" Coach Ditka leaned in and pretended he couldn't hear. "Sorry. I couldn't hear you. My Super Bowl ring was making too much noise!"

Everyone, especially Dad, started hooting and laughing.

After the speeches were over, a group of parents wanted to talk to Dad about the Tigers' losing record.

"I hear your concerns," Dad said patiently. "But for me, it's not completely about winning and losing."

"I agree," said Ambrose's dad. "But we *are* going to win a game eventually, aren't we, coach?"

"We've had a rocky start," Dad had to admit. "But with team effort, we will win some. Well, maybe we'll win some," he added a second later. "But remember," he went on hastily, "there's no *I* in team."

"But there is an *I* in win," Mark's dad pointed out.

Mom tried to defend Dad. "No one else stepped up when the team needed a coach," she reminded the others. "Phil may not be the greatest coach in the world, but at least he's trying."

"I can defend myself, honey," Dad mumbled.

"Do you think he likes losing week after week in front of his own son?" she went on.

"Really, Barbara . . ."

"All I know," Ambrose's father piped up, "is that Ambrose cries after every game."

Byong Sun's mother was concerned about something else. "Are they going to be using their heads, coach? Because Byong Sun still has a soft spot, you know. I heard there's a league in Skokie that has a 'no heads' rule."

"Hey, Weston." Conner's father was next. "What are you doing to improve my boy's skills?"

"I'm trying to instill in the boys a sense of—"

"What is the deal with those birds?" Hunter's mom said abruptly. "I have my hands full with Hunter. The last thing I need is a pet bird!"

A few other parents chimed in, complaining about the birds.

"Okay . . . okay . . ." Dad tried to speak above the noise. "I admit the finches were a bad idea, but we did score a goal today, remember? A real goal . . . an honest to goodness goal . . ."

When the dinner finally ended, Dad was exhausted. He slumped into a chair next to Coach Ditka.

"That was rough," he said. "I wasn't expecting the parents to bombard me with questions like that."

"You did okay," Coach Ditka reassured him.

"I mean, I *really* was not expecting that kind of response. That was intense."

"I hear you," Coach Ditka said.

"I'm glad you showed up," Dad went on. "I can't tell you how much I appreciate your coming tonight. You really got to my dad." He grinned, remembering the look on Grandpa

Buck's face when Coach Ditka appeared in the doorway. "That was so great to see."

"Yeah." Coach Ditka grinned, too. "It was sweet. Your old man is a real work of art. I'll give him that."

Just then Grandpa Buck came over and grabbed a chair. He turned it to face Coach Ditka, and the two of them locked eyes.

Grandpa Buck kept his eyes fixed on the coach's face as he spoke to Dad. "I've been meaning to talk to you, Philly. This Ditka thing. I don't like it one bit."

Dad faked surprise. "What's your problem, Dad?"

"You had to stick it to the old man, that's my problem," Grandpa Buck replied.

"What are you talking about?" Dad asked.

"You had to go to my mortal enemy for help. As a way to get at me."

"Mortal enemy? Come on, Dad," my father said. "That's no way to talk about your neighbor."

"No, Phil, he's right," Coach Ditka put in. "We hate each other. I hated him the first time I laid eyes on him. Before that even."

Dad told me later that the two of them glared at each

other for a long time, waiting for the other one to blink or look away first.

"My hate for you has no boundaries," Grandpa Buck said between clenched teeth. "You had it all . . . 1985 . . . 1986. . . . You gave up on Chicago after that. You went to the Saints!"

Dad tried to break the tension. "Oh, look," he said brightly. "The Cunninghams are leaving."

But they ignored him.

"What are you even doing here, Ditka?" demanded Grandpa Buck. "You're just coaching the team to get under my skin."

"That's right," Coach Ditka retorted. "And it's going to get worse before it gets better."

"Did you pay the check yet, Dad?" my father asked desperately. "And, by the way, did anyone notice Don Flemming? He must have lost twenty pounds."

"Hey, Weston," Coach Ditka was saying. "Why don't you take your pretty young wife and get out of here."

"Whoa!" Grandpa Buck pushed back his chair and stood up. "What did you call her?"

"I'm just saying." Coach Ditka stayed calm. "You've got a pretty wife. Take her home."

"She is the light of my life!" Grandpa Buck shot back. "You don't talk about her like that. And another thing, Ditka: I'll go home when I want!"

Dad panicked when he saw Grandpa Buck moving closer to the big coach. "Guys, you're making a scene."

"Stay out of this, knucklehead," Grandpa Buck warned him.

"Don't talk to him like that!" Coach Ditka growled.

"He's my son, I'll talk to him any way I please!"

"I'm telling you for the last time, Weston," snarled Coach Ditka. "Take a hike."

"Oh yeah?" Grandpa Buck stood toe-to-toe with Coach Ditka.

"Hey! Hey!" Dad cut in. "Stop it. You're acting like children!"

I'm glad I wasn't there to see it. Because the next thing everybody knew, Coach Ditka raised his fist to punch Grandpa Buck—and then my father stepped right between them.

CHAPTER TWELVE

"Look at this, Barbara!" Dad gazed proudly at his reflection in the bedroom mirror. He had a terrible-looking black eye. "I took a punch by Hall of Famer Mike Ditka, and I didn't go down. I wobbled a bit, but I didn't go down!"

"You were unbelievable, honey," Mom said. "So brave."

"You should have seen the look on my father's face," Dad went on. "It was priceless. That punch was meant for him, and I took it! That's what feels so good."

Mom let him go on a little longer.

"Phil," she said finally. "Can we please stop talking about

your dad and Mike Ditka? You need to relax. Coaching this soccer team is making you so tense."

"You're right," Dad agreed. He let her rub his shoulders. Soon he was more relaxed—and sobbing like a baby.

"I'm in way over my head, Barbara," he blubbered. "And I'm scared. Not only that, I got punched in the face, and it hurts! Sam and the other kids don't need me. They need a real coach."

"You're a great coach, Phil," Mom tried to reassure him.

"No, I'm not." He shook his head. "I'm a joke. And I'm sick and tired of my dad teasing me!"

"Well, I love you," Mom said.

"*You* love me?" Dad looked at her, confused. "What does that have to do with anything?"

"That's it!" Mom snapped, annoyed. "I'm done. I've tried to talk to you, but it's not working. You need to talk to Ditka—not me—about all this."

That set off Dad's crying again. "Ditka scares me," he blurted out. "Have you ever looked into his eyes? Or at his hair?"

"He's been a coach for a long time, Phil," Mom insisted. "I

think you need to share your feelings with him."

"You want me to share my feelings of inadequacy with Mike Ditka?" Dad shook his head. "I can't do that. He'll hit me again. And it hurts!"

"I don't think you have a choice," Mom insisted. "It's your only option."

Finally, Dad agreed. "You're right," he admitted with a sigh. "I'll talk to him soon."

"That's great, honey." Mom gave him a quick hug. "But Phil?" she added. "Try not to cry in front of him."

The next day Dad stood in front of a coffee shop with Coach Ditka. I'm not sure how many words Dad managed to get out before he broke down.

Coach Ditka held two cups of coffee as he stared at my father in shock. "Are you crying?"

Dad nodded, tears streaming down his cheeks. "When's the last time you cried?"

Coach Ditka thought for a second. "I don't know. Maybe never."

At that Dad burst into a fresh round of tears.

Coach Ditka pushed a cup of coffee at him. "You've got to knock this off, Weston. We have work to do. Now drink."

Dad shook his head. "I don't drink coffee. It's not good for you."

"Drink it!" Coach Ditka ordered.

Slowly, he sipped. "Mmmmm." He sniffled and then took another sip. "It's good."

"Drink some more," said Coach Ditka. "Then stop crying and tell me what's on your mind."

Obediently, Dad sipped more coffee. "I think I should quit coaching," he said. "I can't do it."

"It's a hard job," Coach Ditka said sympathetically. "When things are going badly, everyone blames you. But when it works, Weston, there's nothing like it."

Dad blew his nose. "Really?"

"Really," Coach Ditka confirmed. "Now no more talk about quitting. We're about three seasons away from turning these boys into a winning team. In fact, we have something to do right now."

Coach Ditka led him down the street to a butcher shop, Pirendello's Meats.

"What are we doing here?" asked Dad.

"Getting some fresh meat," explained the coach.

Inside the shop, meat carcasses hung from hooks. The butcher, Umberto Pirendello, stood behind a tall glass counter. He greeted Coach Ditka warmly.

"Ah, coach! I got your bratwurst ready." Umberto handed him a package wrapped in white paper.

"*Grazie*, Umberto," Coach Ditka thanked him. "Hey, are your nephews around?"

"In back," the butcher replied in his Italian accent.

Coach Ditka motioned Dad toward the rear of the store. "Go take a look."

Dad slowly stepped toward the back. When he peeked inside the room, he saw two small boys packing up meat.

Confused, he turned back to Ditka. "So? Two kids working. What does that . . . ?"

Just then one of the boys ripped off a section of butcher paper and wadded it into a ball. He tossed it into the air, bounced it off his knees several times, and then kicked it to the other boy. The second boy neatly headed it back to the first one, who used his head to knock it into a wastebasket.

"Whoa," Dad whispered.

"Meet Gian Piero and Massimo," Coach Ditka said, beaming.

"They're incredible," Dad murmured. "What are you thinking, Ditka?"

"The Tigers lost Benson's two boys when he stopped coaching, right?" Coach Ditka said. "Umberto's nephews are the right age—and they live in the right district."

Dad nodded eagerly. "Excuse me, sir?" he called to Umberto. "Those two boys? Are they interested in playing soccer?"

Umberto scowled. "Gian Piero and Massimo? They no play. They are my butcher apprentices."

"Oh." Dad was disappointed. "They don't play soccer?"

"Oh, they play soccer like the pros," Umberto corrected him. "But they have too much to learn—the English. And the meat business."

Gian Piero and Massimo came closer, trying to figure out what the men were discussing.

"Why don't you let them play soccer with American boys," Dad suggested. "They'll learn lots of English that way."

Massimo and Gian Piero spoke rapidly in Italian to their uncle for a few minutes.

Umberto hesitated. Finally, he gave in. "Ah . . . okay," he said. "They play so they can learn a little English. But it no can interfere with they work, eh? Work comes first—meat first, then soccer."

"Meat first, all the way!" Dad reassured him.

The boys smiled happily and celebrated with high fives.

Coach Ditka grinned at Dad. "I'm telling you, Weston. Every good thing in my life started with bratwurst!"

Dad and I were downtown, walking along the street, when I first heard the news.

"What do you mean, we have two new kids on the team?" I asked.

Dad explained about Pirendello's Meats, and how Umberto's nephews were helping their uncle in the butcher shop.

"I'm telling you, Sammy," Dad went on, "these boys have real soccer skills."

"Do they speak any English?" I asked.

"They know the words for every cut of meat," Dad replied. "They can learn the rest from you guys."

Suddenly, he stopped short. "What is that haunting

aroma?" he said, glancing around.

It was coming from a coffee shop, Bean Town, on the corner.

"Let's check it out."

"But, Dad . . ." I followed him as he turned around and headed toward the coffee place. "I thought you didn't drink coffee."

"That was before, Sammy," he told me. "But lots of things around here are starting to change!"

CHAPTER THIRTEEN

By the time we played the Generals, my father was completely hooked on coffee. When he showed up at the field before the game, he was holding a huge cup of the steaming brown liquid.

"Okay. Huddle up, everybody. I know we're on a five-game losing streak," Dad said, "but I have good news: We have two new players. Their names are Gian Piero and Massimo."

I looked toward the parking lot. Two small boys, dressed in jeans and T-shirts, were slowly heading in our direction. With them was an older man, their uncle Umberto.

Nobody, including me, was very impressed.

"They're little kids," I murmured.

Mark smirked. "The butchers are here to help us," he joked. "But I guess the blacksmiths and the candlemakers couldn't make it."

Everyone laughed.

"These boys are from Italy," Dad went on, ignoring all the comments. "They don't speak English very well, so we're all going to help them learn."

When the Italian players reached us, Dad introduced them to the team. Umberto told Dad that he would be back at five to pick up the boys.

"Have fun, you two," he told his nephews. "Don't hurt anyone. And remember: Meat comes first!"

"Here." Coach Ditka tossed soccer jerseys to the new boys. "Put these on."

We all watched them slip on the shirts. The boys were so small, the jerseys almost reached their knees.

These are the two kids who are going to save our team? I thought skeptically. No matter what Dad had told me, I didn't believe him.

When we took the field a few minutes later, I heard a few Generals players snicker at our new recruits, too.

Then the game started—and everything changed.

Within seconds, Gian Piero had captured the ball. He passed it to Massimo, who swiftly dribbled it down the field—and right into the goal.

Whoa! I thought. *That was amazing!*

Tigers, 1; Generals, 0.

On the sideline Dad and Coach Ditka were already celebrating.

"Here's the new game plan, Tigers!" Coach Ditka yelled gleefully. "It's called 'Get the ball to the Italians!'"

I stood on the field, watching in awe with everyone else, as the two new boys scored again and again, using their heads, chests, and feet to execute unbelievable moves, like "scissors" and "bicycle kicks." The Generals' goalie never had a chance; the ball was coming at him too fast and too often.

"Shouldn't we give some of the other kids a chance to play?" I heard Dad ask Coach Ditka at one point during the game.

"Hmmm . . . that's a good idea. But let's keep Gian Piero and Massimo in," Coach Ditka replied.

Mark's father overheard them, too. "I agree," he said enthusiastically. "Keep those boys in and pull my son!"

"Dad!" Mark exclaimed from the field.

"I'm just thinking of you. You look tired, champ." Then Mark's father turned back to Dad and mouthed, "Pull him!"

When the ref finally blew the whistle to end the game, I looked up at the scoreboard.

Oh my gosh, I thought.

Tigers, 18; Generals, 0.

We all ran toward the Italians and piled on top of them. On the sideline, Dad and Coach Ditka slapped hands and celebrated, too.

"Seventeen to zip!" Coach Ditka exclaimed.

"Eighteen!" Dad corrected him.

"Keeping score, huh, Weston?" Coach Ditka teased. "Feels pretty good, doesn't it? That's why they call it winning!"

Dad grinned. No matter what they called it, it felt great.

A moment later all the Tigers huddled together. It was finally our turn to cheer for the another team.

"Two, four, six, eight.

Who do we appreciate?

Generals! Generals!

Yay, Generals!"

I ran over to hug Dad. "We won! We finally won!"

Warming the bench . . .

Mom and Dad try to be supportive.

Coaching soccer doesn't exactly come naturally to my dad.

But sometimes his pep talks aren't so bad.

Dad and Grandpa Buck play a "friendly" game of tetherball.

Mom and I are not impressed.

Gian Piero and his brother, Massimo, our Italian soccer stars.

Sometimes we have to help Gian Piero and Massimo out at their uncle's butcher shop so they can play . . .

Grandpa Buck yells at the Gladiators.

Like father, like son . . .

Practice gets intense after Dad recruits Coach Ditka.

Gian Piero and Massimo take it up the field.

Byong Sun takes a shot.

Conner can finally see!

Bucky and I used to be teammates—now we're rivals.

On the field, it's me against Bucky.

He was still grinning. "You'd better believe it, Sam. You guys were just missing that one special ingredient."

"You mean the best coach ever?" I said loyally.

"Please, you're embarrassing me," he protested. But he was loving it; I could tell.

In the distance I could see Grandpa Buck. He'd been watching our game closely with his binoculars. Now, as he lowered them, I caught a glimpse of his face. For the first time I could remember, he looked worried.

Very worried.

CHAPTER FOURTEEN

Thanks to Gian Piero and Massimo, our team shot rapidly to the top of the standings. And while we taught the new kids lots of new English words, they showed us some cool new soccer moves. I learned how to fake right and go left, and how to do a three-sixty move.

One day after soccer practice I bumped into Bucky.

"Hey, I heard you guys won a game," he said.

"We've won five!" I corrected him.

"Great. How many goals have you scored?" he wanted to know.

"Er . . ." I fumbled. "Well . . . none . . ."

"How many have those Italian kids scored?"

"Forty-three," I answered.

"It must be fun to watch," Bucky said.

"It is," I agreed. For the first time since I'd joined the Highland Heights Soccer Organization, I was having a great time.

My father was enjoying himself, too.

The next time we went to Grandpa Buck's house for a barbecue, Dad was in a great mood.

"Smells good out here," he told Grandpa Buck.

Grandpa Buck stood near the grill. "They're sirloin burgers."

"No, I mean the air," Dad said, drawing in a deep breath. "It's a beautiful day. Couldn't ask for a better day. And I'm feeling fully alive."

Grandpa Buck shot him a look. "After you get out of poetry class, I've got a flat of pansies that need planting," he muttered.

"Very funny," Dad replied.

"So how's Sammy doing with the soccer?" Grandpa Buck wanted to know.

"Good. We're having a great time together. The Tigers have won five in a row," Dad couldn't resist adding.

"You mean the Italians and Ditka have won five in a row," Grandpa Buck stated.

"We're five hundred now," Dad said dreamily. "And soon . . ."

"We're a thousand," Grandpa Buck cut in.

"I've got to tell you, Dad, I think the Tigers are going to make it to the finals."

Grandpa Buck laughed hysterically.

"I'm serious," Dad insisted.

"Look, Phil." Grandpa Buck shook his head. "I love you like a son, but it ain't going to happen."

Dad shrugged. "We'll see."

Grandpa Buck narrowed his eyes. "Feeling pretty full of yourself, huh? It looks to me like someone needs to be taken down a couple of notches."

Dad glared at him. "You calling me out?"

"I'm calling you out!" Grandpa Buck confirmed.

"No going back," said Dad.

"You're on!"

Within minutes, the two of them stood in front of the tetherball set, glaring at each other.

Mom saw them and hit the panic button. "No, no, not this!" She hurried over. "What are you two doing? Don't you remember the last time you did this?"

I was nervous, too. Whenever the two of them played tetherball, it was a disaster.

"It's okay, Bar." Dad tried to soothe my mother. "We'll play just one game."

But Grandpa Buck had a different idea. "The best two out of three. Don't worry," he told Mom. "This won't take long. The boy has never won a game against me. Two games, and we're done."

"I wouldn't count on that, Dad!" my father shot back.

"What is the law, Phil?" Grandpa Buck demanded.

"Stop it," Dad warned.

"I said, what is the law?"

"And I said, stop it," Dad replied.

Grandpa Buck finally recited the answer himself. "The law says: You shall never beat the old man at anything."

"Just serve the ball," Dad ordered.

Grandpa Buck served, and the two of them punched the tetherball back and forth. Suddenly, Dad hit it hard. Grandpa Buck dodged out of the way, and the ball smacked Dad hard on the back.

He grimaced in pain.

Grandpa Buck chuckled. "Need a time-out, sonny?"

"Not on your life!" Dad replied.

"I like this intensity," Grandpa Buck taunted him. "You should try bringing some of it with you on the soccer field."

"Grrr!" Dad growled as he smacked the ball back at him.

Grandpa Buck won the first game. Soon after that, I got up and went inside to eat dinner with Bucky, Mom, and Janice. We all knew that it would be a long time before Dad and Grandpa Buck were finished playing.

When we got back outside, the tension mounted as the ball rose higher on the pole.

Sweat dripped off Dad's face.

"You look like you're going to pass out," Grandpa Buck called.

"I'm just hitting my stride!" Dad retorted.

A second later Grandpa Buck punched the ball hard, and I thought for sure the game was over.

Dad missed the tetherball with his hands, but somehow he managed to return it with his chest. "Owwww!" he bellowed in pain. "That smarts!"

Grandpa Buck was a little thrown off by Dad's surprise attack.

Sensing an advantage, Dad started whacking at the ball like a punching bag. Within minutes, it was wrapped completely around the pole.

"I won! I won!" Dad screamed. "Match game. It's one to one!" He tore off his shirt and waved it around, whooping. Angry-looking red welts and bruises covered his chest and back.

"All right already, Phil!" Grandpa Buck snapped. "Don't start celebrating quite yet. I gave you that one! I'm finishing you off here and now."

Dad wiped his face with his shirt. "I'll make this game short and sweet, Pops. Once I start, I ain't stopping. I'm going to hit where you're not."

"Shut up and serve!" Grandpa Buck snapped.

I went in to eat dessert. Meanwhile, Dad and Grandpa Buck kept playing. And playing. They were both exhausted. But neither showed any sign of quitting.

Grandpa Buck suddenly returned the ball hard, hitting Dad right in the face. Blood squirted from his nose.

Mom leaped to her feet. "Phil? Are you all right?"

Dad waved her off. "Don't talk to me right now, Barbara!" he snarled. "I'm fine." Then he glared at Grandpa Buck. "I . . . will . . . not . . . die!"

They kept on playing.

That was when I turned to my mom. "Do you ever ask yourself why—"

"Why I married your father?" she joked.

"No. Why do Grandpa and Dad act like this all the time?" I asked.

"They don't mean anything by it," she answered slowly. "It's just their way of showing they love each other."

"I will stomp on your grave!" Dad screamed a moment later.

Mom and I exchanged grins.

"Your father's a good man, Sam," she went on. "It's just

that Grandpa brings out the worst in him."

"That's for sure," I murmured, gazing at the pitiful figure who was my father.

By now Dad's eye was almost swollen shut. When Grandpa Buck smacked the ball toward him, he was barely able to return it.

"Time!" Grandpa Buck grabbed the ball for a second. "You okay?" he asked Dad.

Dad staggered, trying to keep his balance. "I'm more than okay. *You* called for the time-out, old man." He walked over to a table where Janice had set up a container of Gatorade. He unscrewed the lid and poured the drink all over his face, gulping like a dog.

Then, while Dad slipped off his pants, Grandpa Buck took off his shirt.

"All set?" Grandpa Buck asked.

"Why are you talking so much?" Dad snapped.

At that, Grandpa Buck served the ball.

Dad punched back hard. The ball zipped past Grandpa Buck, then slammed Dad in the back of the head as it wound rapidly around the pole.

Dad got thrown forward, his hair pasted up like a peacock.

"Now I bury you!" Grandpa Buck bellowed.

Dad tried to dive for the ball as Grandpa Buck attacked. But he was too late. He landed hard on the ground, scraping his chest.

He jumped to his feet. His eye was swollen, his arm looked limp, and now his chest was covered with blood.

"I don't believe this," Bucky muttered, looking at me.

I could tell by his face that he was thinking exactly what I was thinking: that his father and my father were nuts—completely nuts.

"Want to go inside and play a game or something?" he asked me.

"Yes!" I declared.

"Good idea, boys," Mom chimed in, looking disgusted. "Whoever invented tetherball never imagined a scene like this, I'm sure!"

After we went inside, Grandpa Buck quickly racked up more points. Mom told me that he pumped a fist at Dad. "This is it, Phil! I can feel it!"

By now Dad's vision was blurry. Dimly he could see the ball arc upward. As it slowed, he set his aim, ready to blast it. Then, with all his strength, he reared back and let out a death scream.

The match was over.

CHAPTER FIFTEEN

"I almost had him, Barbara," Dad murmured a little while later. He was sitting at Grandpa Buck's kitchen table while Mom tended to his cuts and bruises. "It was the best I have ever played against him."

"And it didn't grind the barbecue to a halt or anything," Mom said sarcastically. "Tetherball only took three hours."

Dad finally realized that she was annoyed. Very annoyed. "Are you mad about something?" he asked her.

"You made an excellent impression on your son tonight," she informed him. "Sam and Bucky both want to know what's wrong with the two of you."

Just then Grandpa Buck came into the kitchen, whistling cheerfully. He had showered and changed into a Buck's Sports Town running suit.

"I almost had you," Dad couldn't resist telling him.

"Oh, really?" Grandpa Buck pretended to look confused for a minute. "What's that called again when you almost win? Oh yeah . . . losing!"

They were still arguing a few minutes later when they came into the living room, where Bucky and I were playing a robot game. But now they were fighting about soccer.

"I'm telling you, Dad," my father insisted. "We're making it to the finals, and that's where this is going to end. I'll bring you down in front of everyone."

"Whoa, Seabiscuit. Slow down," Grandpa Buck told him. "That ain't going to happen."

But Dad was all fired up. "You want to make a little wager? A bet between father and son?"

Grandpa Buck thought for a second. "Fine," he said slowly. "Here's the deal: When I beat you in soccer, then you sell that break-even vitamin store of yours and come to work for me at Buck's Sports Town."

"Oh, no." Dad shook his head. "I'm *not* working for you."

Grandpa Buck made chicken sounds. *"Buc—buc—buc."*

"Fine!" Dad snapped a moment later. "But if I win . . ." He looked around, trying to think of something he could take for a prize. Finally, he spotted something in the trophy room— the Pelé soccer ball that Grandpa Buck had snatched from him when he was a kid.

Dad eyed the ball, a gleam in his eye. "If I win," he said slowly, "you have to give me the Pelé ball."

Grandpa Buck blinked. "I have to do what?"

"If I beat you in the finals, then you have to give me the Pelé ball," Dad repeated.

"For the day, you mean, right?" Grandpa Buck said.

"No. Forever," Dad clarified.

"No way, José," Grandpa Buck stated firmly.

This time it was Dad who started clucking like a chicken.

And it was Grandpa Buck who couldn't take it. "Okay, then. We've got ourselves a bet."

Oh, no, I thought.

I glanced at Bucky, who looked just as worried as I was.

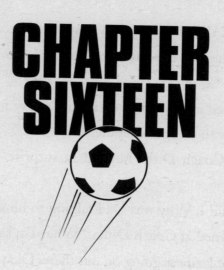

CHAPTER SIXTEEN

After Dad made the bet with Grandpa Buck, he started drinking coffee around the clock. And he wasn't guzzling plain old coffee anymore; now he was sucking up espresso, the really strong kind.

I wasn't the only one worried about him.

"Hey, Phil," Coach Ditka said during warm-ups before our next soccer game. "Your wife told me about the bet you made with your old man."

"So?" Dad was distracted, looking at the game plans he'd drawn up the night before.

"Just don't get ahead of yourself, Weston," Coach Ditka

warned him. "We've had a pretty easy schedule so far. And we have to win the next five games to make it to the semis. Maybe you should—"

Dad looked up. "Maybe you should worry more about the team and less about the schedule," he cut in.

"*What?*" Coach Ditka blinked in surprise at my father's sharp tone.

And so did I. Why was Dad talking to him like that?

Dad frowned at Coach Ditka. "What I'm saying is, there's a whole lot of laziness going on out there. Okay, everyone," he called to us. "Pay attention. This is important."

We got into a huddle. As Hunter joined the circle he tried to slip a candy bar into his mouth.

Dad caught him. "Hunter. Not now. Wait until right before the game. You could use the extra energy. Okay, then, Tigers," he went on. "I called this meeting so we could talk about some of the sloppy play I've been seeing on the field. It seems to me there's a blatant disregard for our game plan."

He held up the board with all his latest diagrams. Big arrows pointed to two marks, which we all knew indicated our two stars, Gian Piero and Massimo.

"Ambrose," Dad snapped. "Last game, I saw nothing but

nonsense from you. What were you thinking?"

Ambrose shrugged. "I don't know."

"That's exactly my point! And Jack, who are you supposed to pass the ball to?"

"Gian Piero and Massimo," Jack answered dutifully.

"Byong Sun." Dad paced around us. "*When* do you pass the ball to the Italians?"

"The instant I come into contact with it," Byong Sun answered like a machine.

Dad stopped and glared at us. "Right. That's our strategy. I would think sooner or later it would sink in. It's one of the many plays we've worked out."

"It's the *only* play we worked out," Mark reminded him.

Dad wheeled toward him. "How many sarcastic pills did you take this morning?"

"I'm . . . I'm just saying—" Mark stuttered.

"No, really, because maybe I should speak to your parents. They should be aware of your dosage."

"Coach—" Mark tried to explain.

But Dad was on a roll. "May I suggest flushing the sarcastic pills down the drain and maybe taking some "coach appreciation" pills instead?"

This was humiliating.

"Dad!" I grabbed his arm. "You've got to lighten up."

"Listen, Sam." He stared hard at me. "I remember a certain boy who was very sad when he lost, and I also remember that same boy and how happy he was when he won."

"Yeah, I get it, Dad," I muttered. "That boy is me."

"And I'm doing all of this for you, Sam. So we can all have fun."

I was about to point out that nobody on the team was having fun anymore when Ann, Byong Sun's mother, approached.

"You're late!" Dad yelled at her. Then he realized she was alone. "You were supposed to pick up Gian Piero and Massimo. Where are they?" he demanded.

She looked upset. "Sorry, coach. There's a little problem."

Dad looked panic-stricken. "Where are my Italians?"

"Working," Ann mumbled. "Umberto received a big order, and the boys have to work all day to help him get it ready. I'm sorry, Phil. There was nothing I could—"

Dad whipped out his cell phone and punched in the number of the butcher shop.

"It's a very important game, Umberto," I heard him say. "We need to win all our games to get to the semifinals. I can't afford to lose a single game. And without Gian Piero and Massimo . . ."

He paused to listen to what Umberto was saying. "No. Meat does not come first. It's soccer. Soccer comes first."

Mr. Pirendello must have hung up at that point. Dad stood there for a moment with his cell phone. Then he started pacing up and down the sideline like a madman.

Suddenly, he stopped. A grin broke out on his face. "You guys wait right there!" he shouted at us. "I have an idea!"

Ten minutes later the entire team had arrived in front of Pirendello's Meats.

"All right, guys, we've got twenty-five minutes—and a lot of meat to cut!" Dad called.

We hurried into the back, where Massimo and Gian Piero had been working all morning.

The two boys handed Dad a tool that looked like a mini chain saw, and he went to work hacking a slab of meat. Blood and bits of meat flew all over the place. The rest of us started picking up slices of meat and wrapping them in white paper.

Meanwhile, Coach Ditka waited at the soccer field, where the coach of the Hammerheads was giving him a hard time.

"If your players aren't here soon, your team is going to have to forfeit," he threatened.

"They'll be here," Coach Ditka promised.

We worked frantically. When all the meat was finally cut and wrapped, Mr. Pirendello raced us back to the field in his meat truck.

As the meat truck screeched to a stop, all the parents and players at the field looked up. The back door flew up, and a cloud of cold air drifted out. Then we all jumped out.

The Hammerheads' coach gulped as he took in our bloodstained uniforms. "What in the world . . . ?"

The players stared at us, their mouths open in terror.

Behind us, Dad jumped out of the truck. Blood and meat dripped from his hair and tracksuit. "We made it!" he called to the Hammerheads. "Sorry we're late!"

He held out a hand to shake with the other coach.

But the Hammerheads' coach took one look at the blood and guts dripping from Dad's hand and shook his head. "We forfeit!" he told the ref.

"We win!" Dad yelled happily.

I formed a circle with the rest of the Tigers.

"*Two, four, six, eight.*

Who do we appreciate?

Hammerheads! Hammerheads!

Yay, Hammerheads!"

CHAPTER SEVENTEEN

"I'm cold, Mr. Weston," Ambrose murmured.

It was the following weekend, and my father had come up with his worst idea yet—a team campout.

He'd pitched several tents in our backyard and built a fire in a big pit. Everyone was complaining about the low temperature as we huddled around the fire, trying to stay warm.

Ambrose's teeth were chattering. "I'm freezing cold, Mr. Weston," he repeated.

"It's *Coach* Weston," Dad corrected him. "And it's not cold, Ambrose."

"Then why did you build a fire?" Ambrose asked logically.

"Fire is the stuff of warriors," Dad informed him. For a second, I thought he was going to jump to his feet and start beating on his chest. "And that's what we are . . . warriors!"

I heard someone say something under his breath. I couldn't hear the words, but I knew they were about Dad—and not very kind.

"But, what are we doing out here?" Hunter blurted out.

"We're bonding," Dad said firmly. "Coming together as a team. Fighting the elements. What doesn't kill us makes us stronger."

"Coach?" Conner was hungry. "Did you order the pizzas yet?"

"In due time, Conner. In due time."

Mark yawned. "I'm getting tired. Can't we take this inside?"

"It's freezing out here," Ambrose said again.

"Please, coach," pleaded another kid. "Why can't we sleep indoors?"

But Dad wasn't about to change his mind. "I'll throw another log on the fire. Fire is good. It's primal. Come on," he urged us. "Let's all bay at the moon."

I stared at him in disbelief. "What are you talking about?"

"You know," Dad said. "We can howl. Like this." Then, to my horror, he stood up and began howling at the moon.

"Coach Weston!" somebody cried out. "What are you doing?"

I was mortified. "Dad, come on. You're scaring us."

He kept howling. Soon several dogs in the neighborhood joined in. The howling grew louder and louder.

I heard a window fly open. "Shut up out there!" one of our neighbors yelled.

"You shut up in there!" Dad screamed back. "I'm baying at the moon!"

I covered my face with my hands as Dad and all the neighborhood dogs kept up the howling.

Why in the world had I ever decided to play soccer?

I wish I could tell you that my father calmed down after our team won the next four games and made it to the semifinals. Instead, he acted crazier than ever.

At practice all he did was yell at us to pass the ball to Massimo and Gian Piero. One night he used Mom's sewing machine to add brightly colored flames to his coaching outfit. And he was drinking so much coffee, the employees at Bean

Town actually threw him out of the coffee shop.

Finally, it was the day of our semifinal match against the Scorpions. We arrived at the field early to warm up and go over our game plan.

But I wasn't the only one starting to get sick of soccer— and of our two star players.

When Gian Piero and Massimo showed up, nobody bothered to greet them.

"Hello, everyone!" Massimo called cheerfully.

There was no reply.

He tried again. "Maybe we go later after a game and get the pizza?"

Silence.

"Or maybe we learn more English?" put in Gian Piero. "I practice good. The English is easy. I am very *ing* about it."

Ing?

We all looked at one another.

"You're *ing* about it?" Mark echoed. "What does that mean?"

"*Si,*" said Gian Piero. "I am *ing*. Like in Italian. *Essere.* It means 'to be.' Like I am. I am *ing*."

Hunter scoffed. "You can't say, 'I am *ing*' in English. You need a word in front of it. Like . . . I am hog*ging* the ball."

"Or," Conner jumped in, "I am not pass*ing* the ball to my teammates."

"Here's another example." It was Mark's turn. "I am annoy*ing* everyone on the team."

We all walked away, leaving Gian Piero and Massimo standing there, baffled.

We warmed up for a while. Then Dad called us over for a pregame huddle. But instead of talking to us and trying to motivate us to do our best and play as a team, he started yelling about how he wasn't going to tolerate any laziness, even if we had a big lead.

Coach Ditka was fed up with him, too.

"Hey, Phil," he spoke up. "I don't think that's the right attitude—"

"You don't *think*?" Suddenly Dad was in Coach Ditka's face. "You don't *think*? Well, I don't *think* you should be butting in when I'm talking to my team."

"It's our team," Coach Ditka reminded him.

"No, it's my team! You're my assistant. You back me up and get the juice boxes when I tell you to. Now go get me a juice box!"

"You're crazy." Coach Ditka stared at him. "Who do you think you're talking to?"

"Number one . . ." Dad held up a finger. "I'm talking to the juice box guy. And number two . . ." He held up another finger. "I'm not crazy. I'm thirsty. Now get me a juice box!" he screamed.

Coach Ditka fumed.

Byong Sun stepped between them, trying to calm things down. "Fellas . . . fellas . . ."

But Dad and Coach Ditka weren't listening. Instead they moved closer to each other, crushing poor Byong Sun with their stomachs.

"Now get me a juice box!" Dad commanded.

Coach Ditka let loose a string of angry words. "That's it!" he said finally. "I'm outta here!"

My heart sank as I watched the famous football coach stalk off the soccer field.

Dad watched him go, too. For a second I thought he might apologize. But I should have known better.

Instead he went after Coach Ditka again.

"You don't have to quit, Mike! You know why? Because you're fired!"

Coach Ditka didn't bother to reply. He just kept walking toward his car.

Dad turned back to us. "I'm only going to allow winners on the field. Who's a winner?"

We all hung our heads.

"Who's a winner?" Dad shouted again.

This time a few kids halfheartedly raised their hands.

"That's what I want to see! Now huddle up. Who are we?"

"The Tigers," we all said without enthusiasm.

"Starters onto the field!" Dad ordered. Then he turned to the parents and beamed with satisfaction. "We're in the semifinals. This is what we've worked for all year."

None of the parents said anything. After hearing him scream at Coach Ditka and us, they were all too stunned to utter a word.

I wasn't one of the starters. I sat on the bench for the entire first half. When the second half began, I got up to ask Dad about going in.

"Dad?"

"Not now, Sam," he said, without even looking at me. His eyes were fixed on Gian Piero and Massimo as they attacked the Scorpions' goalie. "Yes!" he shouted as Massimo scored again.

"Dad?"

"Not now, Sam! My Italians are in destruction mode. Now grab some bench!"

I stomped back to the bench and stared glumly at the field. But I wasn't watching the game anymore.

Finally, the ref blew the whistle to end the game. The Tigers had won the semifinal, 10 to 4.

"Victory!" Dad shouted triumphantly. "We made it! We're in the finals!" He ran onto the field, high kicking and making whooping sounds. Then he picked up one of the orange safety cones and began yelling into it, screaming things at the other team.

I had never been so embarrassed in my entire life.

I got up from the bench and slunk off the field. And right behind me were most of my teammates.

CHAPTER EIGHTEEN

"**W**ow, huh, hon. Wasn't that amazing?" Dad said to Mom as he came into the living room, carrying coffee mugs on a tray.

I'd gone to bed already, mostly to avoid having to talk to my father.

Mom was on the couch, reading a magazine and frowning at him. "You need to stop, Phil. You're going overboard."

He looked at her. "What are you talking about?"

"You called a group of ten-year-olds losers today," she reminded him.

"I did not," Dad denied it.

"You did so," Mom insisted. "You screamed it into that orange cone, and everybody heard you. People three fields away heard you call those kids losers!"

"What do you want me to call them?" Dad demanded. "Winners? That would make me a liar. What is with you and Sam?" he went on. "We're in the finals. Am I the only one who cares about that?"

"Sam went to bed pretty upset," she informed him.

"Upset?" Dad still didn't get it. "We won. We beat the Scorpions in the semifinals. What more does he want?"

"You didn't play him," Mom stated. "I warned you about this, Phil. This soccer team has become all about you and your father."

"That is completely untrue!" Dad said defensively. "And as far as my not playing Sam, it's his fault. He needs to speak up for himself. I'm way too busy during games to worry about every player."

"Sam's not every player," Mom said softly.

Dad frowned. "You're not seeing the big picture, Barbara. We won."

"I'm finished talking to you," Mom snapped. "You're like some kind of animal!" She stormed out of the room.

"Where are you going?" Dad called after her. "I don't understand why you're walking away like this!"

Mom didn't bother to reply.

Now she wasn't speaking to him, either.

Dad actually had a chance to get out of the bet he'd made with Grandpa Buck. He told me later that with both Mom and me mad at him, he decided to go for a walk. Before long, he found himself at the park.

It was dark and the athletic fields were deserted. Dad wandered over to a baseball field and picked up a bat and a few stray balls.

"I'm not an animal," he murmured, hitting balls into the net.

Just then he spotted Grandpa Buck coming toward him. "What are you doing here?" he called, surprised.

"Visualizing," Grandpa Buck explained.

"What?"

"I always walk the field the night before a big game,"

Grandpa Buck explained. "I visualize. I play the whole game in my head. It's like meditation."

He looked closely at Dad. "What are you doing here?"

"Nothing," he muttered.

"Who were you talking to?" asked Grandpa Buck.

"Myself. It's like meditation." He went back to hitting baseballs against the backstop.

"When you were a kid, we spent a lot of time out here," Grandpa Buck said suddenly. "How many grounders did I hit to you?"

"Too many for me, that's for sure," Dad murmured.

"I worked you hard because you had potential," Grandpa Buck defended himself.

"I was just a kid," Dad snapped back at him. "You worked me so hard, it stopped being fun!"

"What are you saying?" demanded Grandpa Buck. "I was a bad coach?"

"No."

"Then what?" Grandpa Buck prodded him. "A bad father?"

Dad kept his eyes off Grandpa Buck's face. "I'm not sure

you really knew the difference."

"Maybe I could have done better in some areas," Grandpa Buck admitted. "But you live and you learn. I'm certainly trying harder with Bucky."

"Listen, Phil," he said suddenly. "I want to let you off the hook."

"What do you mean?" asked Dad.

"When I beat you tomorrow, you don't have to stick to your part of the bet. You don't have to come work for me if you don't want to."

"*When* you beat me?" Dad repeated.

"Yes," Grandpa Buck confirmed. "When."

Dad shook his head. "Do me a favor. Don't be so nice to me. Keep me on the hook. I'm not afraid of the hook. In fact . . . I *like* the hook."

"Look, all I'm saying—" Grandpa Buck started.

"I know what you're saying, Dad." My father cut him off. "Now, if you'll excuse me, I'm busy."

"Son, I just offered you an out from a bet that you can't possibly win. So before you turn down my generous offer, why don't you take the night and think about it?"

Grandpa Buck walked away, and Dad kept on hitting baseballs.

When he looked up a few seconds later, Grandpa Buck had already disappeared into the darkness.

CHAPTER NINETEEN

When I woke up the next day, I had already made up my mind. I had had enough of my father and his stupid bet with Grandpa Buck. And I'd had enough of soccer and sitting on the bench. There was no way I was playing in the championship game against the Gladiators.

Dad left for the field early in the morning. He didn't talk to Mom or me; he just assumed we would meet him at the game.

I heard from Conner and Jack later that there was a lot of excitement at the park before the game started. Parents and players had decorated the field with streamers and balloons, and the eighth-grade band played from the bleachers. Jim, "the Captain" from Captain's Car and Home Audio, had set up an announcer's booth.

"Good afternoon, ladies and gentlemen!" he blared into a microphone. "Welcome to the HHSO championship game. I'm Jim 'the Captain' Davidson from the Captain's Car and Home Audio, and I'll be giving you the play-by-play, blow-by-blow, of what promises to be the biggest game of the year—the Tigers versus the Gladiators."

Everyone said that Grandpa Buck looked as pumped as Dad. On the Gladiators' side of the field, his players surrounded him, hanging on his every word.

"The Tigers are not that good. It's a two-man team," he told them. "You have to stop the Italians. Double up on them. We can do this. I'm very proud of you boys."

On the Tigers' sideline, Dad was pacing—with a huge cup of coffee in his hand, of course. To my surprise, he actually noticed that I wasn't there and called home on his cell phone.

"Barbara?" Mom and I heard him say into our answering machine. "The game's starting soon. Where's Sammy? I thought you guys were going to meet me here."

Mom looked over at me. I was on the couch, watching TV.

"What do you think, honey?" she asked softly. "It is the last game of the season, and—"

"I'm not going!" I repeated for the tenth time that morning. "Dad has the Italians. He doesn't need me."

"Sammy . . ." Mom started to say. But the look on my face made her drop the subject.

At the field I knew that Grandpa Buck and Dad would be warming up their teams. I found out later that they didn't look at each other for a long time. Then, a few minutes before the game started, Grandpa Buck crossed the field to talk to Dad.

Their eyes locked.

"Big game today," Dad said.

Grandpa Buck nodded. "The Captain is doing the play-by-play. It doesn't get any bigger than that."

"What do you want, Dad?" my father asked.

"Just for the record . . . I offered to let you out of the bet, but you're turning me down. Is that right?"

"No. That's not right. The way I remember it, you tried to back out of the bet, and I wouldn't let you. The bet's on, Dad," my father went on. They were still staring at each other. "You gonna break that stare?"

"Nope."

Their eyes stayed locked for a long time. Dad tried to keep his gaze on Grandpa Buck's face, but finally his eyes started tearing, and he blinked.

"Ha!" Grandpa Buck snickered and walked off.

The two teams lined up in the center field as the band played the national anthem.

I'm glad I wasn't there for this moment—apparently my father was singing at the top of his lungs, off-key, and missing most of the words.

The ref signaled for the two coaches to meet at center field for the coin toss.

"Okay, men," the ref said in a warning tone. "I'm watching you. This is a championship game, and I'm going to run a tighter ship than usual. It's my field. I call the shots. Keep your players and their parents in check. Got it?"

Dad and Grandpa Buck nodded. The ref tossed the coin.

"Heads!" Grandpa Buck called out.

The coin landed on heads.

"The Gladiators kick off," announced the ref.

Dad smirked. "Just the way I like it."

The crowd cheered as the Gladiators and Tigers took their positions on the field. A second later the ref blew the whistle.

A Gladiator touched the ball a couple of times. Then Massimo shot forward to steal it. With perfect aim, he passed the ball to Gian Piero, who was waiting near the goal to receive it.

"Wow!" exclaimed the Captain as the ball rocketed into the goal. "The Tigers score with an incredible opening play!"

"Oh yeah!" Dad did a little celebration dance. "Did you see that?" For Grandpa Buck's benefit, he made a big show of checking his watch. "I'm talking about ten seconds into the game. Call Ripley's Believe It or Not! This is going to be the blowout of the century. At this rate, we'll score three hundred goals!" He looked across the field and yelled to Grandpa Buck, "Give up now, Dad!"

"It's a long game, sonny!" Grandpa Buck called back. Then he turned to his players. "Shake it off, boys. One goal. It's no biggie. Line up."

Within minutes Gian Piero had the ball. Quickly, several Gladiators were on him. Gian Piero looked around for Massimo, but three other Gladiators had him blocked.

Bucky seized the opportunity and managed a steal.

"Go, Bucky, go!" Grandpa Buck coached him. "Now! Run the mongoose! Look at that! Go, man, go!"

Bucky broke free and dribbled past Mark's open legs. Quickly, he took a shot and scored.

Tigers, 1; Gladiators, 1.

Now it was Grandpa Buck's turn to celebrate.

"How do you like that, Philly? There's plenty more of that coming your way!"

"Give me your best shot, old man!" Dad retorted.

The Tigers had the ball. Gian Piero passed to Massimo, who was quickly challenged by the Gladiators. He passed to Byong Sun, who stood right in front of the Gladiators' goal.

Byong Sun watched the ball, and then glanced at the net in front of him. Should he shoot?

"What are you doing?" Dad screamed at him. "Pass it off! Pass it off!"

Byong Sun looked toward the right, where Gian Piero stood, open. Then he glanced back at the goal and made a sudden decision.

He kicked the ball toward the net. Slowly, the ball rolled right at the goalie. The Gladiator scooped it up and kicked it out to a teammate on the wing.

"The Gladiators steal the ball!" the Captain announced.

"No!" screamed Dad.

"Yes!" screamed Grandpa Buck. "There's an open field, boys! Take it in."

The Gladiators player passed to Bucky, who instantly fired it into the Tigers' goal.

"Yes!" Grandpa Buck pumped his fist.

"And the Gladiators have taken the lead!" the Captain said into the PA system. "It's two to one!"

Dad was furious. He yelled for Byong Sun to come out of the game.

"What was that?" he demanded.

Byong Sun cowered. "I—I thought I had a shot."

"You *thought?*" Dad echoed. "You pass it off to one of the Italians. That's your only thought! How many times do I have to say this?" he railed on. "During practice you take shots. During games you pass to the Italians!"

Byong Sun slunk over to the bench and sat down.

But Dad wasn't finished screaming. On the field, Ambrose had just tripped a Gladiator, and the ref called a foul.

"A foul?" yelled Dad. "Are you kidding me, ref?"

"Good call, ref. Good call!" Grandpa Buck was saying.

"That was a horrible call!" shouted Dad.

The ref had heard enough. He blew his whistle and then motioned angrily at the two coaches.

"Coaches! Here. Now!"

Grandpa Buck and Dad walked to midfield.

"You guys are going to have to pull in the reins," the ref told them.

Dad nodded. "I'll relax," he promised. "I just wish you weren't so blind."

"I'm warning you!" The ref snarled at him.

"Fine." Dad huffed. "Oh, can I ask you something?" he went on. "How much, ref? How much did my old man pay you to call the game his way?"

Now the ref was really mad. "You are one wisecrack away from being thrown out of this game!"

"Fine!" Dad shouted back. "Can we at least show some enthusiasm?"

"At a respectable level," the ref retorted. "Now back to your places and let's keep the comments to ourselves."

At home Dad left us another message. "Uh, Bar, there's a championship game going on, remember? Where are you? And where's Sam?"

I looked at my mother. "Don't even say it, Mom. I'm not going."

"Sammy." She sighed. "Being mad at your father is one thing. But your team needs you."

"No, they don't," I reminded her. "They have Gian Piero and Massimo."

"The Tigers aren't just your teammates," she went on. "They're your friends. And I'm sure that most of the boys are wondering where you are right now."

I folded my arms and pretended I wasn't listening. But as I turned back to the TV, I couldn't help it. I was thinking about my team and wondering what was happening on the field.

By now Byong Sun was back in the game. Massimo had the ball and was charging toward the goal. The Gladiators' goalie came out of the net to challenge him.

Massimo quickly passed to Byong Sun. The net was still open.

"Kick it!" yelled Massimo. "Shoot!"

But Byong Sun was looking around for Gian Piero, who was on the other side of the field.

"Hey, little one. Kick it!" repeated Massimo.

Some of the other Tigers yelled at him, too. "Kick it!"

Byong Sun stood there, paralyzed. He looked nervously at Dad.

Just then a Gladiators player ran up and lunged for the ball. He knocked into Byong Sun, who went down hard.

A few minutes later, when the first half ended, Byong Sun was still lying on the field.

Dad ran out to him. "Byong Sun, are you okay?"

"My leg . . ." he moaned.

"What were you doing out there?" Dad asked. "What were you waiting for?"

"I was waiting for an Italian. Pass the ball to the Italians. Isn't that what you always tell us, coach?"

Dad didn't say anything. He just nodded. Conner and Ambrose came over to help Byong Sun across to the sideline.

A few minutes later Mom and I arrived at the field.

"There you are!" Dad hurried over to us, looking relieved. Then he glanced at me and frowned. "But, Sam, why aren't you wearing your uniform?"

I ignored him and kept walking toward my teammates.

"What's with him?" Dad asked Mom. "And where have you two been?"

"I'm surprised you noticed we weren't here," Mom said dryly.

"I noticed. I called you twice. Is Sam sick?"

"He's not sick," Mom replied. "He didn't want to come. It took me all morning to convince him. He finally agreed because he thought it was important to support his team."

Dad glanced over at me. "He doesn't want to play for me?"

"He'd love to play for you, Phil," Mom snapped. "But you've embarrassed him—and turned him into a bench-warmer. Sound familiar?" she added hotly.

"I . . ." Dad fumbled. "I . . . was just trying to get to the championship, Barbara. I didn't mean . . ."

"Well, you're here," Mom retorted. "Take a look around. I hope you like what you see."

Dad glanced around at the field. Byong Sun was on the ground, rubbing his leg and crying while his mother tried to comfort him. A bunch of pumped-up fathers were

126

barechested, each one with a letter painted on his chest to spell out Tigers. Hunter was madly shoving candy into his mouth, his face smeared with chocolate. Across the field, Grandpa Buck was yelling at his team.

And then Dad's eyes focused on me . . . sitting in the bleachers in my street clothes instead of my soccer uniform.

CHAPTER TWENTY

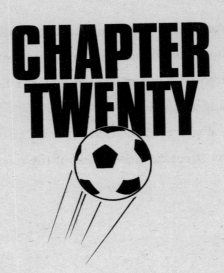

"Hey, Sam." Slowly, Dad walked over to the stands where I was sitting. "Can I talk to you?" he asked, sounding nervous.

I shrugged. "I guess." I kept my eyes away as he sat down next to me.

"Grown-ups are always telling kids when they mess up," he started. "But the truth is, sometimes grown-ups mess up, and they don't have anyone there to tell them about it." He paused, then added, "I messed up, Sam."

I couldn't help being sarcastic. "You think so, Dad?"

He nodded. "I got too caught up in . . . everything. But I

get it now. I lost my way, Sam. If you give me another chance, I'll make it up to you."

I stared at him. Dark circles rimmed his eyes, making him look very tired—and very sad. I wanted to stay mad at him, but I couldn't. In fact, I felt a little sorry for him. He'd been acting like a total jerk, and now he knew it.

"Okay," I said softly.

"What?" Dad said, surprised. "Then you accept my apology?"

"Yep."

"Thank you, Sam." He put an arm around me. "You're starting the second half. I'm going to rest the Italians for a while."

"What? You're not going to play the Italians?" I couldn't believe it. "But, Dad, aren't you worried about losing the game?"

"Nope." He shook his head. "I'm more worried about losing you."

"Oh, man." I grinned. "Don't go all Oprah on me."

He grinned back. "Go suit up."

Mom was standing nearby. "I brought your uniform, Sam. Just in case."

Dad hugged me, and then I ran to the restroom to put on my soccer uniform.

While I was getting changed, Dad talked to the rest of the team.

"I owe you guys an apology. Truth be told, I've been . . . well, a bit of a jerk."

"I'll say!" Ambrose piped up.

Hunter faked a cough, and then muttered something under his breath.

A few other kids chimed in about how nutty Dad had been acting.

"We didn't even recognize you anymore," said Conner.

Dad took it all in. "I get it now," he said, nodding. "And you're right about all of it."

"Hey, Dad." Just then I ran up to join them. "The second half is about to start."

"Oh." He glanced at the field. "One more thing, guys: It's come to my attention that I forgot to play our subs in our last game. I'm sorry about that. So in the second half, we'll start the game with you guys. Gian Piero and Massimo, you guys played your hearts out. Why don't you rest for a bit?"

They looked relieved. "Thank you, coach! Thank you!"

"Let's win or lose this one as a team," Dad went on. "What do you say?"

We shouted our approval.

"Okay. Everyone's hand in the center. On three. I'm sorry, and I hope that one day I can make it up to you." He began counting. "One . . . two . . . three . . ."

"I'm sorry and I hope—" everybody started to repeat.

"No!" Dad laughed. "Not that."

I jumped in with a new chant. "Tigers! Tigers! Tigers!"

Soon the whole team was cheering.

"Tigers! Tigers! Tigers!"

The Tigers players took the field, with Gian Piero and Massimo sitting on the bench. The Gladiators quickly got possession of the ball—and began to dominate us completely.

I admit it; I started to panic.

I waved frantically to get my father's attention. "Dad! You made your point. Now put the Italians back in!"

"It's okay, Sam," Dad said calmly. "You guys are doing great. Stay with the ball, and keep working together."

On the opposite side of the field, Grandpa Buck was loving it.

"Yes!" he yelled as he watched his team take control of the game. "This is the intensity I've been looking for, boys!"

The Gladiators scored. Now they were beating us, three to one.

"Come on, Tigers. Trust your teammates. You can do it," Dad encouraged us.

After the Gladiators' goal, we kicked off. A Gladiator quickly stole the ball. He passed it to a teammate, who shot it toward the net. Conner tried to make the save, but as usual he dove in the opposite direction from the ball.

The ball went wide of the net. Conner looked over at Dad, plainly upset.

"Injury!" Dad yelled at the ref. Something had suddenly occurred to him. He spun toward the parents on the sideline. "You, you, you, and you . . ." he said, pointing to the ones wearing glasses. "Give your glasses to me!"

The parents looked confused, but they took off their glasses and handed them over.

"Thanks!" Dad ran toward Conner. Quickly, he held up a pair in front of the goalie's eyes.

"Is your vision better or worse?" asked Dad.

Conner hesitated. "Ummm . . . a little better."

Dad held up another pair. "Better or worse?"

"Worse," Conner replied.

Dad showed him another pair. And another.

"That's better," Conner finally said. "I can see much better with these glasses on."

"That'll do then," Dad replied.

He ran off the field. "He's okay," he told the ref.

I grinned as I saw the ref shake his head. He wasn't sure what to think about the eye exam Dad had just given Conner.

The ref blew his whistle and the game started again.

Conner picked up the ball and booted it toward Mark. One of the Gladiators immediately stole it away. Conner braced himself as the Gladiator charged the net.

This time Conner dove right at the shot. He stared down at the ball in his hands, amazed.

"Good save, Conner!" said Byong Sun.

"Way to go!" I cheered him.

"Dude," yelled Ambrose. "You needed glasses!"

Conner's save was just what our team needed. Conner kicked the ball to Mark, who took it down the field, getting past several Gladiators.

Gian Piero and Massimo shouted at him from the bench: "*Il collo! Il collo!*"

"Huh?" Mark was confused.

"On your neck!" the Italians shouted. "Use your neck!"

Mark nodded. Now he got it. It was a trick they had taught us.

Mark kicked the ball up toward his neck and raced with it down the field. When he was close to the goal, he let it drop.

"Ambrose!" Dad shouted. "It's time for a power kick."

On the field the rest of us formed a flying wedge.

Ambrose charged toward Mark like an angry bull. He kicked the ball out from between Mark's legs and aimed it toward the goal.

Score!

Tigers, 2; Gladiators, 3.

I glanced over at the Gladiators' sideline. While our team celebrated, Grandpa Buck frantically coached his players.

"Go back to our regular play!" he told them. "Forget what we practiced, okay?" Then he turned to look at Dad. "What was that, Phil? You're pulling your star players? That's playing right into my hands, son!"

"I love you, Dad," my father screamed back at Grandpa

Buck, who didn't seem to know what to make of Dad's new coaching strategy.

Next it was Hunter who surprised us all.

A Gladiator passed the ball to a teammate. But before it reached its target, Hunter, holding a candy bar, came out of nowhere. He stole the ball and ran it down the field. Then he passed it to Jack.

As several Gladiators closed in on him, Jack closed his eyes. He kicked the ball toward the goal.

Ambrose stood in front of the net. He held up little Byong Sun like a battering ram. Then he used Byong Sun's head to butt the ball right into the net.

"Holy cow!" shouted the Captain from the announcer's booth. "The Tigers have come back and tied up the game. This is unbelievable!"

I looked at the scoreboard.

Tigers, 3; Gladiators, 3.

Grandpa Buck fumed. "We are not losing this game!" he screamed at his team. "Do you hear me?"

Dad turned to Gian Piero and Massimo. "I want you guys to go back in," he decided suddenly. "But remember: This time it's not about the Italians, it's about the Tigers."

Gian Piero nodded.

"Got it, coach," said Massimo.

On the field Massimo quickly got the ball and ran toward the goal. Suddenly, he stopped and stepped over the ball. He kept running, flaring to the left. The ball sat waiting for Mark, who took it to the right. Then he, too, stopped and stepped over it. Another player took over.

One by one, each player on the field executed his part in a play we had learned called the "Blue Angel."

Grandpa Buck didn't know what to do. At first he told his players to stick with the Italians. Then he realized what was going on.

"No, it's a trap. Stay with your man!" he shouted frantically.

When it was my turn to take the ball, Bucky was there, waiting for me.

"You're not getting by Uncle Bucky," he said softly.

I grinned at him. "Here's something your father never taught you."

With that, I spun my body into a perfect three-sixty move, whirling past Bucky and carrying the ball toward the Gladiators' goalie.

I faked right, and then aimed the ball toward the left side of the net.

Goal!

Cheers rang out on the Tigers' sideline.

The ref's whistle was already in his mouth when he glanced at his watch to check the time. He gave three short blasts, and then it was all over.

I ran toward my father, who was coming toward me with a huge grin.

"We did it, Dad!" I said, hugging him tightly. "I can't believe it! The Tigers won the championship!"

CHAPTER TWENTY-ONE

All the Tigers and fans were going crazy. Kids were hugging each other while their parents and people in the stands cheered: "Tigers! Tigers! Tigers!"

Not far from where I stood on the field, Dad was helping Bucky get to his feet. As I watched them, a thought suddenly came to me: *Had Bucky let me get by him to score?*

No way, I told myself a second later. There was no way a kid as competitive as Bucky would throw a championship game—even for his nephew.

The Captain was shouting into the PA system. "This

is truly the upset of the century! The great Buck Weston has been dethroned—by his son!"

Grandpa Buck shot the announcer a dirty look.

"Oh . . . sorry," the Captain tried to apologize. "Great game, Buck."

But Grandpa Buck had already stomped over to yank out the plug to the sound system.

Just then my teammates surrounded me. Together they lifted me high, then carried me off the field. After they'd set me down, Grandpa Buck came over.

I was worried that he was going to be mad at me for scoring the final goal.

"Sorry, Grandpa," I said quickly.

But he shook his head. "Are you kidding me? If anyone was going to beat me, I'm glad it was you. That was a great shot, Samson."

I was still worried. "You're not mad?"

"The only thing I'm mad about is that I let you get away from my team."

He gave me a kiss.

As I watched him walk away, though, I could tell he was

at least a little angry. I heard him curse, and then I saw him smash his clipboard over one knee.

Oh, well, I thought, grinning. My grandfather would always be very competitive. And now I knew why: It felt great to be on the winning team.

The next day Grandpa Buck invited us over for a barbecue. Bucky had invited some kids from the Gladiators, and just to show what a good sport he was, Grandpa Buck had invited some kids from the Tigers, too. I spent the afternoon showing Bucky and the other Gladiators the three-sixty move that Gian Piero and Massimo had taught me.

While the kids played soccer, Dad and Grandpa Buck did what they always did: They argued over how to grill the meat.

"That one needs to be turned, Phil," Grandpa Buck said, pointing to a burger.

"Looks fine to me," Dad shot back.

"I'm telling you . . ."

At the house next door to Grandpa Buck's, a leaf blower suddenly started up.

"Ditka!" Grandpa Buck barked.

"Dad, relax," my father said. "I'll handle it." He hurried

over to the fence while Grandpa Buck took over at the grill.

"Hey, Coach Weston," Mark called to Grandpa Buck. "Remember when we beat you for the championship?"

"Yeah," Grandpa Buck replied. "That was yesterday."

"Yeah, remember?" Mark said, grinning slyly.

But Grandpa wasn't going to fall for it.

"Remember when I pushed that kid in the pool?" he said. And then, before Mark realized what was happening, he lifted a foot and knocked Mark into the water.

We all laughed as Mark splashed around. "Okay . . . you got me," he admitted. "That was a good one."

As Dad approached the fence, Coach Ditka turned off the leaf blower.

"Hey," Dad greeted him. "We won the championship. Look, Mike," he added quickly. "I'm sorry. I didn't mean—"

"Listen," Coach Ditka cut in. "I never quit on anyone, but you were a maniac."

"Yes." Dad had to agree. "I was a maniac."

"But I heard you finally came to your senses," Coach Ditka went on. "Whatever path you had to take, at the end of the day, you did a nice piece of coaching."

Dad was surprised—and touched—by the professional

coach's praise. "That means a lot coming from you. So . . . can I count on you joining me again next year?"

"No way!" Coach Ditka said forcefully.

"Okay." Dad knew better than to push it. "But you and I are good?"

"We're good." Coach Ditka nodded. "How about you and your old man?"

Dad thought for a second. "We're better, I guess," he answered.

"You know, I mean no disrespect to you," Coach Ditka went on, "but I hate that guy more and more each day."

"I know." Dad sighed. Then he brightened. "Hey! I'm about to make good on that Pelé bet with him. Want to come over and watch?"

Dad laughed as Coach Ditka shook his head.

"Nope. I want to get these leaves over on his side before nighttime."

Dad returned to the grill, where Grandpa Buck was busy flipping burgers.

"So Dad," he started. "I hate to bring this up. I mean, I know it's kind of a sore subject for you . . ."

Grandpa Buck knew just what Dad was trying to say.

"Hey. We had a bet. You won fair and square," he said generously. "Good job." Then he reached down under the table and removed a soccer ball. "Here you go, son."

Dad was stunned by how gracious Grandpa Buck sounded. "Dad . . . I'm . . ."

"Look. I know I don't tell you this, but you really stepped up. I'm proud of you, son."

There was a lump in Dad's throat. "Thanks . . ." he murmured, looking down at the soccer ball. "This is so . . ." That's when he realized something.

"Wait! This isn't the Pelé ball!"

"It most certainly is," Grandpa Buck insisted.

"I've been staring at that ball for thirty years. This is *not* the Pelé ball. This one is brand-new!"

"Yeah, okay," Grandpa Buck admitted, "but it doesn't make me any less proud of you."

"I want the real ball," Dad insisted.

Grandpa Buck scowled. "What are you saying? The gesture isn't enough?"

"Look!" Grandpa Buck's wife, Janice, said. She came over, carrying another soccer ball. "Look at what I found in the laundry room."

Grandpa Buck snatched it away from her.

"Dad! Give it to me!" my father shouted.

"No!" Grandpa Buck said stubbornly. "It's mine!"

Dad reached for the ball. The next thing I knew, he and Grandpa Buck were rolling around on the grass, fighting over the Pelé soccer ball.

This time even Mom couldn't stay on the sidelines.

"Get it, Phil!" she was screaming. "Get that ball! You earned it!"

Somehow Dad managed to pin Grandpa Buck and was frantically trying to get the ball away from him.

The other kids and I watched the two of them for a few minutes. Then I did the only thing there was to do—I jumped on top of them. A second later, the rest of the soccer players joined the pile.

"Bucky! Sam!" Grandpa Buck yelled at the top of his lungs. "Set up the tetherball. This doesn't end here!"

At that, I burst out laughing. The soccer season had ended, but the competition between my father and grandfather was far from over. No matter what season it was, the special way that Dad and Grandpa Buck "showed their love for each other" would go on . . . and on . . . and on. . . .